A Retiree's Diary

Year 2024

Roger A. Page

Copyright 2025
Roger A. Page
Independently Published
All Rights Reserved
ISBN: 9798306579450

I was slouched on the couch in the early hours rereading a book I remembered from clear back in high school, John Steinbeck's classic, *The Winter of Our Discontent*. Steinbeck has as few rivals now as he ever did at storytelling, so for my own good I have made peace with him, shelving my dissent for his gross falsities about hunters in *Travels with Charley.* He and I are on firmer footing now that I have resigned myself to reading only his fiction—which as it turns out is all he truly wrote anyhow. It was a good choice, I would hate to cheat myself out of Steinbeck's renowned character, Ethan Allen, entering the High Street Coffee Shop and ordering from waitress Annie, an old girlfriend of his to boot, coffee black... "black as the eye of despair." I drink my coffee black, too, so I paused my reading long enough to copy the metaphor which I intend to use more than just here. As Kipling says, "Words are, of course, the most powerful drug used by mankind."

Back to *The Winter of Our Discontent*, at a point building up to Ethan's taking a crack at robbery he remembers his Aunt Deborah like this:

"Ethan, that outlandish thing could well become your talisman."

"What's a talisman?"

"If I tell you, your half-attention will only half learn. Look it up."

So many words are mine because Aunt Deborah first aroused my curiosity and then forced me to satisfy it by my own effort. She cared deeply about words, and she hated their misuse as she would hate the clumsy handling of any fine thing.

I am always fast to applaud those who care deeply about words. Even as our numbers dwindle, the desire to develop a principled ability toward what Theodore A. Rees Cheney put forth as, "*Getting The Words Right*," is forever to be a championed as a highly redeemable skill, and particularly when advanced to artistry.

I go back and reread many classics, nursing on occasion a desire to bask in the exact artistry mentioned, even as I tend to comparatively, myself, abuse it now and then. It's a sign of the times, as they say. Many of today's modern written words are squarely aimed at spontaneous combustion of emotions and I confess to loving it that way. The profanity, in-your-face humor, political dogma (if it suits me), and other matters of prose which refined authors of yesteryear knew to sidestep are now fair game. I must believe such suppression was torturous back in their day, but tough beans, y'all had your chance.

I'm joking, of course. The point is today's writers are correct to loosen the parameters to fit the times, even as we deplore much about what has become of them. For my own part, I want to assure readers about my overall commitment to words with the allowance of how aware I am of my own sporadic misuse, which nine out of ten times is intentional if you want the whole truth. With that confession on the table, I give you a clearer picture of myself... and am okay with that. I'll have to trust how you choose to see it.

On my own behalf, then, it seemed a good idea, before I get started on another year, to blend Steinbeck and Cheney in representation of what Rudyard Kipling told us about words, and as a sign of the times, advancing my own version—that getting them right is not always a matter of artistry.

I herein set off confidently to demonstrate.

Where we hike, the rustic trails meander without design, all we care about is they ascend and descend enough to keep our legs feeling young. By we, I am including the ever-present hound, currently Audrey, now heading toward twelve years old. But in the past, Tina and Daisy, as well, each left their impassioned pawprints across every inch of the abundant sprawls of woodlands near our home. As years have turned to decades, each time a dog and I leave home for the woods we might seem blithely unaware that our only destination is our next step, but without fail we always appreciate how logical it is for us to keep going.

After a couple seasons of Retiree's Diary now completed, and why I begin this one with mention of hiking with hounds, is that I perceive my own trails ahead much akin to the repetitive and well-traveled thematic pathway that led me here. Without question, and here I am speaking about aging, two of the most essential energies left to propel me onward are those ongoing hikes alongside willing hounds, and secondly, to remain eagerly enthused about getting words onto paper. In each case, whether traipsing the hillsides or camped at a keyboard, may there continue to be nothing in the way I am inclined to step around—rather, let me fervently look forward, as I always have, to every new step while hoping with every fiber of my being that hounds and readers will always want to keep coming along.

Contents

Introduction..10

January

January 03—Medical Notes..14

January 06—"The American People" 23

January 10—Farewell To An Icon 25

January 12—Miracles 33

January 22—The War On English Resumed 37

January 31—In Five-Hundred Words Or Less.................41

February

February 08—Marriage Stories Appendage 5 51

February 12—Super Bowl Observations 52

February 14—Facebook Observations 55

February 15—Songs For Springers 58

March

March 01—That's A Wrap 63

March 04—Blue-collar Versus Office Workers................64

March 07—Marriage Stories Appendage 6 70

March 18—Marriage Stories Appendage 7 75

March 21—Happy Birthday, Audrey Girl.........................77

April

April 01—April Fools' Day...80

April 06—Stories That Write Themselves........................82

April 16—White Rural Rage?..91

April 27—The Actual Threat To Our Democracy 100

May

May 02—This Bridge 107

May 18—The Preakness Miracle 111

May 25--Flags 115

June

June 03—Hockey Parables 122

June 24—Trolling For Bluegills—No, Really...................126

July

July 04—Independence? For Whom? 130

July 11—*Storyworth* Part Two 132

July 19—Fence Sitting?..136

July 30—Dumb Phones?..140

August

August 01—Destination Anniversary 143

August 26—National Dog Day 156

September

September 01—Comes A Time, Reprise........................164

September 02—Labor Day 167

September 10—Marriage Stories Appendage 8............170

September 18—Ordinary Mornings 172

September 28—Marriage Stories Appendage 9............173

October

October 01—What Gene Hill Said 178

October 23—Another Year Distant 181

October 26—Perspectives Of High School Coaching.....181

November

November 09—Forty Years Sober 186

November 13—Déjà vu All Over Again 187

November 28—Thanksgiving 202

December

December 08—Marriage Stories Appendage 10 207

December 18—Seasons End 211

December 19—Marriage Stories Appendage 11 215

December 25—Merry Christmas 218

December 31—Resolutions Ongoing 224

Introduction

I like becoming an old man. You can play around with it almost expertly, milking the daylights out of dwindling expectations, but if your knack for philosophy has kept any sort of pace through the years, now is the time for it to bear its finest fruit.

On the other hand, meaning when I was young, the word crapshoot never had it so good, and, yes, some of my youth indeed required escaping. That seemed awfully dire and drastic at the time, overwhelming even, but I hadn't yet mastered much philosophy. Now when I look back, all that stuff was probably more a matter of procession than it ever was of desperation.

As to this quest to command good philosophy, I hope to get half as good at it as one of my favorite go-to's, Gene Hill. See what you think.

"An old friend of mine used to go out in the mountains every couple of years and just wander around until he was lost. He'd spend a couple of days sorting things out and then settle down. At least that's what he told everyone. Now I'm beginning to wonder what it was he went to lose and what he hoped to find.

Who doesn't have a lot of questions he'd like to have answered? And who else can answer them better than he can, privately, alone, all by himself?"

Hill's old friend wasn't lying. You can develop a deep trust in the solitude found out of the way once you know enough to go there, and especially to go there enough. Throughout my adult lifetime, and particularly as an old man, I have continuously sought and found my own share of answers—privately, alone, all by myself. And now, the older I get, although the questions are less intrusive and answers less complex, I am still energetically motivated to disappear just to hear them anyhow. Never sleight the worth of philosophy; it is a very nourishing pastime.

Specifically, as I set sail to hopefully add this year's book to the growing collection, and due much to that collection itself, I like becoming an old man better than ever. Days seem a little more worthwhile when you are keeping a keen eye out for what you want to say about this or that, it keeps you aware, something old folks need to stay practiced at, evident by so many of my own lapses—or, blessings in disguise, as they are known round here, being the breeders of unprompted stories—lots in the pages ahead. Fortunately, in the general sense, I am thus far only minorly slacking in the head, more in the funny stages than in the sad ones. So, pressing onward, be it exploiting the milking of dwindling expectations for all they are worth, or sometimes disappearing for extended interludes to sort things out, or squaring off against complexities, travesties, or follies, it is solidly armed with willingness and an enviable measure of ongoing zeal that I saddle up for this year's edition of *A Retiree's Diary*. It is especially pleasurable to find you riding along.

January

January 03—Medical Notes

You start right out laughing at the stereotype of old people conversing first about the weather and next about their aches and pains, their meds, their doctor appointments, their latest finds to comfort their aches and pains and then back around to the weather. I promise not to trivially indulge, but you could hardly call it good that over the holidays I went and fired my longstanding primary-care NP after she treated me like a cardboard box (for the final time) when I ran into her at Wegman's grocery store. All I did was try to innocently strike up a brief, amiable, conversation like I do with anyone else I run into in a grocery store, and despite the lady's renown aloofness I expected at least a quick cordial back and forth—after all, it is the holiday season. Karen observed the brush-off from a short distance, and I must add how she did so with a coy smirk. Remember Karen works at Guthrie Medical so knows this NP well enough to reliably surmise what would come next; it's something we had been discussing for quite some time.

"I told you a long, long, time ago to ditch her," Karen grinned upon my retreat.

Immediately upon arriving home I booted up my laptop, clicked on the e-Guthrie page, and canceled every upcoming appointment scheduled with my old Primary Care NP. Next I scheduled an appointment with a new doc who would be a better fit. Here would be the time, too, to mention that my Primary Care NP was not the only storm on the radar. Already logged into my e-Guthrie connection, why not review *all* my upcoming appointments and see about doing a general cleanup? Long story short, I rode my sour mood and wound up laying waste to every appointment on the docket. There. Three of the appointments had to do with that dermatology nonsense I told you about in last year's book, along with two others with my now ex-primary-care NP. Overly ambitious, in my hardline haste I, by accident, axed an upcoming audiology appointment that I promptly reestablished—cannot be dicking around with those.

I won't fault anyone for admonishing me as a supposed loose cannon, it's okay, I'm going to regain your trust later in this chapter, anyhow; but first, it gets worse.

Besides my ex-Primary Care NP and the dermatology newbie with a lust for pincushions, I recently saw a urologist who scheduled an MRI for a more focused look at my prostate based on a rising PSA. I took that darned seriously and readily complied. Afterward, I was surely relieved to see the results showing minor if any concern. During our appointment, the doc had projected some potential scenarios, one being a biopsy if the MRI showed need, which thankfully the MRI did not. On the contrary, the MRI decisively nullified any need for further action at this time. Nonetheless, three days following the results I stepped head-on into an ambush out at our mailbox in the form of a package from Guthrie Medical containing, are you ready for this, a complimentary "Enema Kit."

Pretty easy math, I returned inside where I booted my laptop for confirmation, opened my e-Guthrie account where, sure enough, I discovered an appointment benevolently scheduled on my behalf for a prostate biopsy down in Sayre, Pennsylvania. An appointment made minus any input from me, an appointment made despite the doctor's own standards deeming further action at this time unnecessary, but most of all, a presumptuous act which I slam-dunked with a rapid double-click, "Cancel This Appointment."

Whenever a patient dares to buck their system, Guthrie demands a viable reason and forces the unruly patient to select from a handful of their own cherrypicked options, none of which read, "*Because I never made the fucking appointment in the first place.*" They, in fact, never seem to offer *any* correct answers so I have learned to forgo formalities and breeze straight to the comment section where I always hit the send button before I probably should.

Okay, now the good news: It is well documented how much I owe to many of Guthrie Medical's specialists, accommodating nurses, and other staff, for keeping me alive and functioning, first through my bout with cancer, and a couple years later outfitting me with a new knee. I think the world of those people and always shall, so to balance against all I have said thus far, let me paint a rosier picture of what type of patient I am when treated forthrightly and given mutual respect. Everyone who knows me has heard me shout accolades toward Doc Austin, Nurse Jill, and the physical therapist team of Tom and Sarah, all of whom aided in getting this knee of mine back in order. I complied with all of them along the way because to a tee their combined expertise acknowledged, then encouraged, and ultimately applauded *my* input as significant in accelerating my recovery. That is not merely me boasting; those words are straight from Doc Austin and PT's Tom and Sarah.

But if I were to select the one doctor who would most convincingly testify to my capabilities as a reliable patient, it would be the one most instrumental for my still being here, Doctor Sussman.

I want you to hear our story.

Doc Sussman is a no-nonsense type and many patients of his which I have met along my way opine unfavorably about his blunt "bedside manner." Frankly, I likely would have felt the same had we only one or two encounters—I really didn't care for him at first, but at the time I was not trying to make friends anyhow; Doc Sussman is the one who originally diagnosed my carcinoma. Step two demanded him to perform a non-invasive surgical biopsy to confirm his findings. On the morning of the biopsy an expressionless Doc Sussman entered the staging room where I was being prepped for the O.R. Karen was sitting nervously alongside my bed when Doc Sussman entered and when he disregarded her presence I abruptly interrupted whatever he had begun to say.

"Doc, this my wife Karen sitting here, and she has a lot riding on all of this, so would you please say hello to her?"

What could he do but oblige, and afterward I politely and sincerely thanked him in a good-natured manner so to keep the peace, but I have always believed that brief interjection to be a pivotal moment between us. Whether either of us knew it at the time, those were our first steps in forming a longstanding alliance sustained by an inseverable mutual respect. For the rest of my life, I shall applaud Doc Sussman for his non-defensive reaction to my request that morning.

In a nutshell, doctors Sussman, Collier, and Gosain, along with nurse Karena, were the major players in my battle versus cancer and impending recovery. But far and away my most intense and lasting connection, especially during my years of follow-up, was between Doctor Sussman and me.

Once I had managed my way past the tough stuff and had at last regained my stride toward resuming a normal life, I met with Doc Sussman every four months for routine monitoring. After three years our schedule eased to once every six months.

The air was generally light and believe this or not, I even had him joking and smiling a bit. I openly despised his endoscope even as I conceded its importance. An endoscope consists of a nearly invisible tube to be run through your nostrils clear to your throat where a microscopic camera checks things out. If you know what a "gag reflex" is, you can better understand why Doc Sussman would prefer that I "just relax" when he was probing me with the thing. I hung tough the first time or two but as our relationship developed I felt easier about making clear I would never be "relaxing" for krisesake when it comes to an endoscope. Hoping to solidify my point I asked, "Have *you* ever had that wretched thing rammed up *your* nose, Doc?"

My hopes in scoring an impression flopped big-time.

"Oh, Roger," he scoffed. "You have no idea how lucky you are having a skilled physician administering the endoscope. Back in med school we used to dick around with those things all the time as part of our drinking games."

Wow! From prick to standup comedian!

Our most honest conversation occurred during the early stages of the Covid Games. Doc Sussman predictably lined up on the side of "vaccinating" and at the end of one appointment asked if I had been vaccinated.

"I'm not getting any injections, Doc," I stated flatly.

Doc Sussman instantly ceased notetaking and wheeled my way to forcefully admonish my own bluntness.

"You have to get vaccinated, Roger. You're a sixty-five-year-old cancer survivor. You can't be fooling around with this stuff."

"I have no intentions of fooling around with it, Doc. That's my point. I don't trust the coercive nature of the proponents, and I fully *do* trust a survival rate exceeding ninety-nine percent. I'm not taking any injections."

It escalated, I'm afraid. Doc Sussman echoed the popular, "follow the science" narrative, selectively championed by anyone immune to the fact that the science was, in fact, all over the map, yielding yet more justification for skepticism. The science I was following came from exceptionally trustworthy sources who warned *against* injections. The voices presenting my choice of science were highly credentialed, carried tremendous respect, and wielded the consistency of a survival rate surpassing ninety-nine percent. Plus, and this is no mere sidenote, I had promised Karen. Doc Sussman and I parted that day on uneven terms, that's saying it mildly, but sometimes between people on the same team things nonetheless can get a little rough. After he gruffly exited the room I hadn't realized, I guess, how turbulent our back and forth had gotten until Doc Sussman's nurse, Crystal, with whom I carry on a great friendship to this day, stepped back into the office to set up my next appointment. She was beaming ear to ear.

"Jesus," she said, "Thanks for the entertainment. We could hear you guys clear out in the waiting area."

"Yeah, I suppose we got a bit enthusiastic, but I'm not doing it. I don't trust an injection being called a "vaccine" with only a few months in development. There are gonna be problems, Crissy, I'm sure of it."

"They're gonna *make* us take it," grumbled Crissy. "And it pisses me off because I do *not* want it. I'm the only one here who hasn't quit or caved yet. I keep hoping they'll drop the mandates."

By the time our next appointment came around, the dust beginning to settle on the Covid dogma due to vaccine casualties steadily mounting, Guthrie had instructed their personnel to refrain from initiating any further discussion about injections. Nonetheless, I approached the appointment a shade apprehensive about our heated exchange from last time. Not to worry, though. Doc Sussman entered the office with two interns in tow and introduced them. Then he said this to his interns (and I think to me, too): "Roger is one of our biggest success stories. He has been put through the wringer and has fought his ass off. He's one of the toughest guys you'll ever meet."

I cannot begin to tell you what it meant to hear those words from Doc Sussman. But when he turned to me and added, "Would you please be good enough to share your story with them?" I felt my lips quiver with emotion, a tear rolled down my cheek, and I simply nodded that I would. Doc Sussman turned away quickly himself to leave the room, and it took several seconds for me, the "toughest guy they'll ever meet," to dry my eyes and gain my composure. I then looked each intern directly in the eye and said, "Before I get started, and you can tell we're on emotional turf here, I want each of you to know how privileged you are to be shadowing one of the greatest doctors... one of the greatest *men*... to have ever graced the medical profession."

For the duration of my appointment, then, I shared with them the skeletal version of my journey and concluded by assuring them their chosen field of oncology might be perhaps the most noble quest in the entire field of medicine. We should all applaud those who willingly dare the mire of sadness which comes with the territory, but more importantly, I implored the two young interns to always, *always* remember, too, the lives they will be saving.

My next appointment would be my last with Doctor Sussman—he had announced his retirement. By now, although the Covid Games smoldered as scorched earth, we were all still tiptoeing in lingering foolishness. Hand shaking remained frowned upon, even condemned, in favor of the meek supplementary elbow bumping. Yeah, no thanks. I'm a huge advocate of the firm handshake and as Doc Sussman and I concluded our affairs I took an additional moment for the occasion.

"First Doc, of course I want to thank you for everything you've done for me, but what you did during our last appointment, giving me a chance to impact those interns, is a badge of honor I promise to carry to my grave."

"Well," and here he seemed nearly subdued, "You've taught me some things along the way, too, Roger. I'm not sure how much I'll miss you, though," he chuckled, "but I will. Congratulations on how far you've come."

And with that he turned to the door.

"Doc. Wait a sec," I said. "I'm not about to let the man who worked so hard to save my life walk outta here without shaking his hand."

He turned to face me, slipped his plastic gloves off, and with a melancholy grin gripped my hand tightly and added a soft pat on my opposite shoulder as an exclamation point.

So... you see? As far as being a cooperative and sensible medical patient, all I ask of those judging, is that you weigh the version of me that you think Doctor Hal Sussman would tell.

January 06—"The American People"

In keeping with a medical theme, it seems smart for our nation to undergo what equates to a "physical exam" each year, which we do, but I suggest we move our annual State of The Union appointment ahead to this date where instead of a prepared coercive sales pitch we are instead forced to heed the glaring red flags of how destructive lying and deceit can be to a country's overall health.

"The American People" is a political catchphrase portraying us as one—we aren't—but in the certain instance of January 06, 2020, we can indeed be lumped as such. On that date The American People, every one of us, were lied to and our intelligence mocked.

How sad that so many of America's people continue to fall prey to selective optics evoking the insidious narrative of "insurrection." Equally sad is the way honest American people seem to think striking back with shaking fists and Facebook memes are means of gaining ground. If ever a modern date exemplified The American People as a divided mess being led by political strategists, January 06, it is.

Whenever politicians or pundits declare to speak for, "The American People," as an entity, they defy a defaulted impossibility. "The American People," vary to indefinite degrees and never line up in full support of anything. We the people would be wise to call out such patronization. Anytime anyone claims to speak for The American People collectively, it is a sales pitch. We are nowhere near an aligned society, which above all is a good thing.

The problem in America these days is the liars have seized command. Through aggression and collective bullying, their march for full control of *all* people is clipping along at warp-speed. Meanwhile, more honest folks seem oblivious to the futility of countering the assault by posing conclusive evidence. "We have the evidence right here," say the good guys, while night after night on the news, day after day in classrooms, courtrooms, and city streets, "the evidence" is laughed off as the forage of fools. Year after year powerful tyrants increase their stronghold. Make no mistake, The American Liars do intend to meld The American People into one.

I won't rail for pages, but each year on this date I shoulder my patriotic duty to, if only at my keyboard, remain unsilenced. Whether I make any external impact who knows, but I will never tire of trying to head off America's liars. It is beyond maddening to see *any* of The American People, and especially multitudes, acquiesce to coercive authority rained down from sources aching to command the forfeiture of freedom.

January 10—Farewell To An Icon

Lightening things up, one thing a whole bunch of American people cannot get enough of is the National Football League. Every season millions upon millions of us dig out our fan gear and gather with our own to scream, shout, and holler on behalf of our teams. Karen and I have cheered Seattle's Seahawks for eons, and here would be the time to commemorate the recent glory years masterminded by Seattle's longstanding and highly acclaimed head coach, the energetic seventy-two-year-old, Pete Carroll, who a few days ago announced his retirement.

Personally, NFL football has been a mainstay for as long as I can remember. My allegiance soared into full flight way back when I was a kid in Southern

California during the late 1960's when my brothers and I regularly attended home games of our beloved Los Angeles Rams, played in the fabled Los Angeles Coliseum.

The Rams head coach in those days, the legendary George Allen, was a hero in our household and when Rams owner, Dan Reeves, fired Allen, my brothers and I joined in a local revolt. When Allen departed for Washington to coach the Redskins, he dragged along with him droves of other ex-Rams fans. Right away Allen garnered great interest by developing a roster of such loveable old veterans the Redskins became immediately coined, "The Over The Hill Gang." Allen was additionally able to grab enough of his Ram's players to perpetuate a secondary temporary moniker turning the Redskins into the Ramskins. Great times, for sure, and during his tenure Allen did take the Redskins to a Super Bowl but came up short against the undefeated Miami Dolphins.

When Allen's NFL coaching days ended I opted away from the Redskins thus entering a multi-year abyss of having no team to root for.

In 1976 two expansion teams entered the NFL, The Tampa Bay Buccaneers along with the Seattle Seahawks. I thought little of it at the time but over the course of the next few seasons I peculiarly found myself pulling for the Seahawks at every turn. When, after only a few years into their fledgling existence, the franchise announced the hiring of no-nonsense Chuck Knox to be their head coach, I jumped fully aboard. That was a long time ago.

Carroll's arrival came fourteen years ago, a year after the retirement of hardened veteran head coach Mike Holmgren. When Carroll was announced to the helm of Seattle I was surely not alone in skeptically rolling my eyes. Carroll, after a short stint in the NFL, dropped down to the NCAA college level where he amassed incredible success at USC, winning two national championships there. Carroll's overriding enthusiasm and rah-rah style of coaching proved immensely effective in motivating impressionable college kids but try that act in the NFL. Holmgren had taken Seattle to its first Super Bowl and we fans had grown accustomed to the bottom line—a lot of winning. With Carroll coming to town, I envisioned an atmosphere of scissor-kicks and pom-poms with fans yelling in unison, "We've got spirit, how 'bout YOU?"

... Foolish me.

As it turned out, Karen and I, along with all the rest of Seattle fans, were about to embark upon some elite NFL football seasons. Over the past ten years the Seattle Seahawks are the winningest team in the NFL's National Conference, they went to two Super Bowls, winning one and losing the next with one lousy play to live in infamy; a play that would have been revered as sheer genius had opposing cornerback Malcolm Butler not stepped in and intercepted the ball to secure yet another Super Bowl win for the New England Patriots. Pete was not very popular after that call, but here I insert a quick note to critics—passing the ball for touchdowns from the two-yard line happens multiple times per week across the league. Hindsight tells us it

turned out to be the worst decision in Super Bowl history and I have not once heard Carroll say a word to deny it. He shouldered full responsibility knowing critics are rarely married to reason, so why bother? The fact is, it was a *good* play call, *poorly* executed, and thwarted by an *exceptional* defensive play. Period.
Knowledgeable NFL fans know to shrug and lament, "Hey, it happens," simple as that—even on the biggest stage on earth.

    Like all Seahawks fans, I'd prefer to talk about the year prior to that fabled goal line fail. In February of 2014, the Seahawks faced the daunting Denver Broncos in Super Bowl XLVIII. The 2013 Broncos came heralded as the most prolific offense in NFL history and were led by idolized Hall of Fame quarterback, Peyton Manning.

    During the midweek pre-game interviews, Seattle's quirky running back, Marshawn Lynch (nicknamed, Beast, for a better picture), refused, per usual, to be seated for any questions on media day. Because Roger Goodell's NFL forbids players to make their own decisions about such matters, any player opting out of media day is subjected to heavy fines. Lynch showed up, but barely. He hung back in the shadows, casually leaning against the wall of the tunnel leading out to the field. This made him technically accessible, but his getup leaned toward incognito, revealing his clear intentions to avoid the hoopla. Only through the keen eye of highly revered ex-NFL player, turned NFL Network analyst, Deion Sanders, were fans afforded an impromptu interview. Sanders spied Lynch tucked away from the limelight and cautiously approached. I am not convinced anyone except Sanders would have tried such a stunt, but as he inched forward, Lynch received the noted Hall of Famer with due respect and a relaxed smile. Deion then eased into an unrehearsed back and forth, player to player, man to man, wherein he probed Lynch about the imposing opponents upcoming for Super Bowl Sunday. I will never forget how my own confidence ballooned during the brief dialog. When Sanders said to Lynch, "It's on your back, man. They feel like if they can stop you they can stop this team."

"Nah, they're gonna have to stop *all* of us," stated Lynch determinedly. "I'm a piece to it, but we got some dogs," and the glint that shot from Beast's eye on the count of "dogs," elevated my hopes exponentially.

Turns out, Beast nailed it.

As for the game itself, Seattle had long since retired the number 12 in honor of us fans and for good reason. Without any argument, Seattle is the loudest and toughest venue in which road teams must try to function. But the Super Bowl was played three-thousand miles distant, in New York. What the Broncos were entirely unprepared for, and even Seattle fans could not have realistically seen coming, was the crowd noise in a neutral site raining down so that on the very first play from scrimmage Manning needed to move in from his shotgun position to get closer to his offensive line to relay a change to the original play call. As he neared his offensive line, Denver's center, Manny Ramirez, having no inkling of Manning's intentions, snapped the ball back to where he presumed Manning awaited in his shotgun position. Worldwide, then, astonished football fans gasped as the ball sailed over Manning's shoulder and flew clear through the endzone so before the clock had even begun to tick the Seahawks were on the board with a two-point safety. Later footage would reveal Manning and Ramirez hashing it out on the sideline and lip readers had no trouble sorting out Manning and Ramirez each pointing to the crowd noise as the issue.

For brevity and to resist overtly gushing, it is enough to say how steadily the tone throughout the game stayed true to Seahawks fans. Here in our living room Karen and I watched tentatively at first, fearing at any moment the greatest offense in NFL history could ignite and explode, but when Percy Harvin received the opening kickoff of the second half and rocketed eighty-seven yards right straight to the endzone to make the score 29-0 we eased back enough to realize even the great Manning and the most prolific offense on planet earth were not going to stop the Seattle Seahawks today—no way.

The pundits, experts, and fans, had it all wrong; instead of an offensive extravaganza presented by the Denver Broncos, it was, instead, the Seattle Seahawks defense, flaunting their famed Legion of Boom secondary, opportunistic linebackers, and relentless pass rush, who piled on yet more evidence to support the football adage—offense wins games; defense wins championships.

For a coup-de-grace, late in the third, Seattle's popular quarterback Russell Wilson dropped back from Denver's twenty-three-yard line and hit Jermaine Kearse with a fairly pedestrian completed pass. But Kearse, sensing his own piece of history a mere ten yards away, barged onward knocking orange jerseys from his path like a predator swats flies on his way to the endzone making the score 36-0.

Game over.

In our living room the tears burst forth, Karen and I locked each other up in a victorious death grip and I repeated four, five, maybe six times, "This is really happening, it's really happening..." and so it was.

The final lobsided score was 43-8 and believe me the tears stayed right on track as one Seahawk after another hoisted the Lombardi Trophy. When the cameras caught Pete Carroll spotting his wife Glena trying to forge her way through the frantic crowd toward the podium, he, too, erupted into a meltdown of rare emotions, even for him. I felt good for him, I felt elated for the players, the team, the fans, and when the Beast, Marshawn Lynch finally clutched the coveted trophy in his hands to admire it I thought back to his pledge made to Deion Sanders midweek when Sanders afforded Beast his space away from the crowd. When Lynch subsequently assured Sanders, and the world, "Come gametime, I'll be there," he meant every word.

The following Wednesday, an estimated million people lined the streets of Seattle to share in the utopia of their Seahawks parading the Lombardi Trophy. As I watched the parade on television, and for days after the victory, the reality of it all was still sinking in—a monumental occurrence in Karen's and my lives.

In a follow up story of its own, she and I were in Seattle the next season to share in the mania that the Seahawks have brought to the city's football fans. Before going, wanting to learn how to secure tickets, I contacted a local Seahawks fan I had been introduced to and before we hung up on the phone he said, "Roger, believe me; once you get inside that stadium and hear it for yourself, the rumble you'll feel in the pit of your stomach never goes away."

Correct.

Back to Carroll's retirement, for many recent seasons the Seahawks have grown lackluster. For the past five seasons Seattle has been anemic on both sides of the ball on third downs, they have continuously turned conservative inside the twenty-yard line (red zone) settling for annoying field goals rather than celebrating touchdowns, and what drives us fans maddest of all is that every single season Seattle is among the top two or three penalized teams in the NFL. Perhaps given a bad season or two these stats could be explained and tolerated, but when it happens season after season despite different personnel plugged in at all levels the common denominator boils down to the head coach. So, yes, I have admittedly been hoping for Pete Carroll to step down for the past two seasons; but now that he has, it is nonetheless sad in many respects. The truth is, I do not envy the next in line to come to

Seattle intending to fill Carroll's shoes, particularly from a standpoint of popularity; but I darned well do expect to see some of these recurring problems finally addressed.

In time...

For now, the thing to do for Seahawks fans is to bask in all that Pete Carroll has done for The Emerald City. For Karen and me, we shall forevermore savor the treasure of having been a part of the Pete Carroll era, and more importantly, what an impact those seasons imparted upon the two of us as football fans.

January 12—Miracles

As long as we are talking NFL, come back with me to those days I just told you about when my brothers and I routinely attended Los Angeles Rams home games in the world-renowned Los Angeles Memorial Coliseum, a host venue for two past Olympic Games and slated again for the Summer Games of 2028. Next, if you are hearing it for the first time, my brother Lynn was a quadriplegic, a result of his own horrific football injury back in high school.

There were four of us brothers at the time. First came Jake, the oldest, then Lynn, a couple of years younger, then a lag of thirteen years before my younger brother Ron and I had arrived. Here was the arrangement. We owned two season tickets up in the stands where Jake always sat with either Ron or me; Lynn, on the other hand, in his wheelchair, was afforded seating right down at field level where an accompanying attendant had to join him—Ron and I took turns. A roped off area designated as the wheelchair section was set up on the Ram's side of the field and if I'm even close, the range of the area spread from, oh say the twenty-five yard line down to the ten or so, depending, of course, on the number of wheelchairs. Each wheelchair person was, of course, accompanied by a friend or relative who were seated in one of those cheap ass metal foldup cafeteria type chairs; you know the ones.

Enter the New York Giants in November of 1968, and what a barnburner of a football game did unfold. The Giants jumped out to a fourteen-point halftime lead and we can only surmise the chatter in the Rams locker room, but it surely did matter. Rams quarterback Roman Gabriel stepped out onto the field for the second half and launched a sixty-yard homerun ball to shifty wide receiver, Wendell Tucker. The next time the Rams gained possession, Gabe came through again, this time with a nineteen-yard scamper of his own to get the game tied going into the fourth quarter. In the fourth, the Rams at last seized control when running back Tommy Mason plunged in from two yards out to put the Rams ahead at last. The home crowd buzzed in anticipation of victory, but with only forty-two lousy ticks remaining on the clock, Giants quarterback, Fran Tarkenton, right out in front of our wheelchair section, delivered a bullet to wide receiver Aaron Thomas for an eleven-yard touchdown to tie things at 21 each.

It's been a long time, but what follows is my best effort to reassemble those final forty-two seconds.

Gabriel right away got busy driving the Rams down the field, which, if you're paying attention, translates into the action moving further and further away from our end of the stadium so if you see what's coming, please know I am not here to ruin it. The place was bedlam. Gabe had moved the Rams rapidly down the field and coach George Allen took his final timeout with mere seconds remaining. Tense players now crowded the sideline in anticipation of the upcoming field goal try by reliable kicker, Bruce Gossett, to win the game. As the players inched forward it robbed the wheelchair section of any view whatsoever. This was far before the advent of jumbotrons, no iPhones for a quick live look-in, nothing; I'm afraid the view for those in wheelchairs today was completely blocked so there we all sat totally screwed… well, there *they* all sat screwed. Me, I turned to Lynn and said, "I'm outta here," and sped toward the Olympic track that stretched behind the Ram's sidelines hoping to see Gossett drill this game winning field goal. Adjacently, I heard, "Me, too," followed by a whole chorus of able-bodied malcontents. Everything, so far, about this mass exodus is expected but let's call it utterly jaw-dropping that the fastest among us, sprinting past me and leading us all in our frantic surge down the Olympic track, raced the guy who had until now spent the entire game sitting in a wheelchair a few seats down from Lynn and me.

Allow me just a sec here to interject how us brothers had all entertained this same idea, who wouldn't, but we lacked balls enough to pull it off. Lynn did own a spare wheelchair, and we even got it out once to pump up the tires, check all the working parts, and had everything in order should we choose to take advantage of the lenient wheelchair policy at the Coliseum. That way all four of us could sit right down on the sidelines, right? But when it came right down to it... well... kriste, who could possibly sink to such unscrupulous measures? Tell that to the resurgent fella laughing and speeding ahead of everyone down the track.

When Gossett split the uprights for a Rams win the victorious celebration erupted and I joined the resurgent fella, free now from the confines of his wheelchair, in leaping up and down, gleefully pumping our fists, and triumphantly screaming at each other, "He did it! He made it!" in a display of healthy youthful euphoria. Next, I hurried to make my way back to Lynn to tell him all about it and found him, amid the disarray of scattered metal chairs left askew among the remains of the recklessly dissembled wheelchair section, rocking back and forth in uncontrollable laughter along with the rest of the legitimately handicapped Rams fans marveling at the vacated wheelchair left in the midst of a game winning field goal.

Need a minute?

I imagine the L.A. Times Monday morning edition pumped out the captivating headline, *Rams Win In Last Second Thriller*, accompanied by a photo of Gossett booting the ball; but as a storyteller, I have always wanted that headline to instead read, *Miracle At The Coliseum,* scribed above a photo of an empty wheelchair. Guess you can't have it all.

January 22—The War On English Resumed

I learned the hard way when my neighbor got upset with me and plastered my Facebook Timeline with a meme in replication of a law enforcement badge that read, *Grammar Police—Here To Correct And Serve*. I can't remember details, but I must have overstepped in joking about some minor grammatical infraction— who knows. What I do know... now... is what a grim fate awaits those who are adept at the rules of our language but fail to shoulder our assumed burden of knowing to back off in public arenas. Heaven knows, pomposity is the real sin, not illiteracy. I wanted to feel unduly accosted but the swift raining of laughing emoji's and "likes," collectively inferring gross callousness on my part sunk that ship leaving me the one now upset, so I typed my reply:

Whoa—jeepers. Sorry, everyone, I didn't realize I was being such a stickler. If y'all wanna be drawin' on cave walls, okay wif me... fuckers.

My finger hovered over the send key long enough for a vengeful laugh but for the betterment toward world peace I deleted it and have not since corrected anybody's grammatical atrocities and won't, no matter how abject.

I am unhappy about not fighting back but it's of no use. Here, however, with an audience I can trust to be sympathetic with my fragileness in seeing our English Language shot full of holes, I feel safer and among friends. I am not embellishing any of what follows. These are word for word Facebook posts, none of which I dared contest.

I carry sarcasm around like house keys, don't ask me nothin dumb

When this hit my Facebook page I busily and repeatedly typed versions of, "*It is impossible to ask someone nothin dumb, especially someone so dumb they can't master a period,* but my own retorts left me handcuffed as yet more sarcastic than the original perp. It's maddening, but the right thing to do is to refer back to a saner meme: *Take a hint from your dog—kick some grass over that shit and move along*; so delete your comment before it stirs yet more shit.

Look, typing and deleting what we otherwise fantasize posting is a widely used form of peacekeeping. You have probably done it, too, but I honestly do not know whether to ask for your sympathy, empathy, or prayers, in helping me to resist blowing up my whole network of friends as I grow closer and closer to unleashing.

Here's one. If the meme itself doesn't threaten to break you, the two immediate comments will.

People don't care what you goin thru as long as you ok enough to come thru for them.

Comment #1: Well said!

Comment #2: Perfectly said!

The advantage of knowing you will likely be deleting your comment is it nullifies the need for any toning. But one of these days, I'm telling you, *one of these days*, I am not going to delete a single word nor exercise one iota of caution. I turn giddy dreaming of that day despite knowing, well said or even perfectly said, it will spell my own doom.

I'm going to let you play/ Ima let u play:

i love a man who is patient with me cause I do be on one sometimes

Before, in your own mind you respond, be aware that nothing is a misprint—the leading i is not capitalized while the second I is, and, per usual, periods are extinct.
What did you come up with?

Risking the assumption it's a she performing the meme, I want to know how patient she will be when roles are reversed and he be the one who's on one? We all want people to be patient with us when we do be on one sometimes, I'm sure, but being on one can entail numerous and varying scenarios, some of which call for more patience than do others... I'll stop—this sort of ranting does me no favors, but, come on, what does "on one" even imply here?

How about this one:

IDC if u a Supervisor, Sun Visor, Advisor, or a Budweiser, U gone talk to me like u got some sense!

Alright, I'm laughing, I admit it, I'm only human. The off-the-wall inclusion of Budweiser is what did it for me. Sure, there is a lot wrong here, but who can disparage an overriding cleverness and despite no calling whatsoever for an exclamation point, just to see *any* punctuation at the end of a sentence is a real treat!

I know I am validifying my neighbor's Grammar Police criticism of me, so let me balance things out a bit. This was posted by a younger friend of mine who struggled for an agonizing spell after his last breakup, so we were all happy to see him, at last, land upright. So far, so good, in that relationship, and it was a joy to see this placard posted amid the general melee.

I didn't live a full life until I met you. You make my life happy because you're everything to me.

Word for perfectly scribed word, this meme, presented by my friend, Tommy, to his new love, Kara, spilled straight from the heart. So, you see, it can be done, even in earnest.

We should move along but who cannot see a round or two more upcoming? Until then, I wish to hold the fort with an eye-opening meme which surgically turned the tables and laughed back at me.

Don't blame the clown for acting like a clown. Ask yourself why you keep going to the circus.

I took it well, offered no plausible retort being there is none, full confession: I *love* these things, so I humbly rested back on my comfy sofa and chuckled to myself, "Well said... *Perfectly* said."

January 31—In Five-Hundred Words Or Less

Keeping with words and language, another thing I learned the hard way were the stringencies about word-counts when I first began pitching magazine articles. My first published article was for *Bear Hunting Magazine*, a magazine I didn't know existed until seeing it advertised on a hunting forum. A story I had written about arrowing my first black bear was worth a shot so I emailed it to editor, Bernie Barringer, who stunned me by replying within the hour saying he could use the story in a certain section of the magazine... *if* I could shrink it to a thousand words.

A thousand words?

Having never worked at storytelling from that angle I had to boot up my story to find out I currently stood at twenty-eight hundred words. Yikes. But here was my legitimate chance to declare myself a published writer, so I needed to pull this off. I had always, it seemed, been aware of the phrase made popular by William Faulkner, *"Kill your darlings,"* but had never felt need to deploy it. The phrase is literary tough love, making it easier, or at least doable, to murder those precious turncoats before they do us in first. A bloody rampage thus ensued, carnage smoldered to ashes, but before the hour was up I triumphantly rose from my keyboard and quipped to Karen, "What a brief career *this* is gonna be." But it worked. I had laid waste to enough of the original story to have my article accepted, picture included.

Magazine submissions are the only times I strictly knuckle down about word-counts, but the practice has proven invaluable from the standpoint of concise editing. It is always advisable to sustain a wary eye for darlings that need killing.

I'll ask you to hold the thought of word-counts while I set up part two of this.

Unlike magazines, full length books allow a writer to freely meander as I now shall. I want to tell you about a generic book publishing plan targeted primarily for elderly folks. It's a cool idea, too, one my sister-in-law, Cheryl, brought to my attention, called, *Storyworth*. It's an alluring format, a selective Q&A mapping that systematically results in a finished book. In a nutshell, for a price, a younger family member, or a gathering of them, entrust *Storyworth* or a common competitor (There are several—*StoryCorp*, *Storii*, *LifeArk*, and I am certain many others, and yet more coming) to format and publish a keepsake vanity book for families who desire a lasting heirloom. Set in motion, the publishers collaborate with family members to formulate a monthly questionnaire which is then presented to the eventual "author," generally an old-timer who is asked to select what questions they wish to answer and disregard the rest. The duration of the project is a fiscal year over which the compilation amassed will be produced into a book; nothing approaching brick and mortar by any means, but otherwise very nicely bound with an impressive hardcover, and all-in-all, a fashionable piece of memorabilia. Extra copies are available but can be costly. I did not delve deeply enough to serve up precise details but have provided enough for you to take up the chase from here.

When Cheryl told me about *Storyworth*, curiosity steered me there to look at some of the questions. Obviously, for a self-publisher the *Storyworth* format isn't necessary, but snooping around for some stimulating fare shouldn't hurt. I visited the *Storyworth* website and opened some "sample" questions. Filing through the questions, seeing a few I wouldn't mind having a go at, I had the brainstorm of limiting myself to a word-count, say five hundred words, answering a few. These days I am amply experienced and fully familiarized with what five hundred words looks like, so it seemed a lenient enough challenge to prevent too many of my darlings from being slain. Plus, it provided a few stories I may not have dug up on my own.

How it went:

Question: *What habit do most people have that you find very strange?*

No hesitation. I find it very strange to see people crossing days off a calendar at day's end—as in, "There, another one bites the dust," in likeness to a morose victory dance, the coup de grace coming from a black sharpie pen slashing a bold X on the calendar before shutting out the lights. The psychological undertones... yikes. Please don't hate me for wanting to suggest an alternative. Maybe at day's end, take a deep breath and rest your sharpie at bay for a sec while affording a few moments to sit quietly and contemplate more deeply about the day you're about to ax. Maybe reflect on something that made you laugh, try to pinpoint the highlight of the day, if you are the praying type, or even not, pause for a few seconds to bid thanks for another day granted. Here is an idea—rather than a gaudy X each day, why not jot a word or two that counts, "Trudy came in today," "Billy and Ally engaged!" "Lunch with Sandy," stuff like that; in other words, *substantiate* each day rather than expunging it as dead and gone—good riddance.

Do you see what I am saying?

Our yesterdays, whether fondly recalled or brutally slain, are what ultimately define us.

(*212 words*)

Question: *Are there any funny stories your family tells about you that come to mind?*

Yep.

How I singlehandedly dismantled the Santa Claus myth.

To qualify for toys at Christmastime, our family had two rules—you had to have been a good boy throughout the year, and you must be asleep on Christmas Eve when Santa arrives. So, there I lay at two AM, having to pee so badly I clutched myself awkwardly while desperately fighting to hold my eyes closed tightly enough to bluff Santa should he show up right now. My sister, Rita, in the room adjacent, heard my unrelenting discomfort so came to investigate. Rita was twelve years old, up to speed, so convinced me to trust my chances—she would keep a lookout... whatever good that would do. I put my faith in her, raced to the bathroom, and it all worked out.

Or so I thought.

A few hours later, Rita, letting our mom sleep in, guided my younger brother and me down to the living room to see all our toys.

Our staircase was constructed as an "L," an upper flight of stairs and a lower flight were separated by a small landing. The upper flight was a walled corridor but once you turned the corner to the lower flight the view encompassed our entire living room. It should have been an innocent prank when my sister suddenly halted as she rounded the corner of the landing and drew back in startled surprise, feigning to have disrupted Santa in the middle of dropping our bounty.

She thought it funny as hell, and my younger brother, Ron, caught on right away, but I was not about to have made it this far only to get screwed. Face it, I was already on the bubble with the "good boy" requirement, having recently got going with my newfound breakthrough of the "F" word, and although none of my higherups had yet caught me, only a fool could believe Santa hadn't heard. There were other things, too, but I had already used most of my five hundred words when I wheeled frantically and tore back up the stairs flunking my getaway at the last step where I tripped and spontaneously screeched a high-tenor f-bomb hopefully doused quickly enough by the clamor of rocketing headfirst into hallway cabinetry. My impact rattled the entire household and dislodged, too, the old-fashioned telephone. Remember the ones back in the day that when crashing to the floor left a residual Ka-WHANNGGGGG—NG—NG—NG... Yeah, those.

Showstopper.

No way Santa is forgiving such folly.

As I lie there squalling in defeat, sister Rita hurried to my side to lend comfort. When she escorted me downstairs my eyes ballooned to see my lineup of new toys after all, a happy ending. But bet your ass in the aftermath, I was far enough along to put two-and-two together—Santa Claus is *not* the one who brings these toys, is he?

(*480 words*)

Question: *When in life have you felt most alone?*

(Lying on that floor moments ago leaps to mind.)

The answer depends upon which version of "alone" is being implicated; the nearly desolate loneliness I felt in my youth at the lowest point in my lifetime, or the highly sought version here decades later. May Sarton, a devoted "loner," said it this way in her book *The House By The Sea*, published in the early 1900's. "Loneliness is the poverty of self. Solitude is the richness of self."

In the first case I was very young and entrapped by self-imposed yet seemingly inescapable failure. I stayed drunk a lot, sometimes high on pills, a compulsive liar, but worst of all I inwardly did little to dispute the certainty I would never amount to a hill o' beans. Utilizing my restricted word-count as an excuse, I'll leave it at that, except to add how painfully some of those memories will always lurk. That I opt against added details should reveal enough.

The alone I want you to know more about occurs often these days, fortifying my penchant for desired interludes of solitude. What I think about while I fish on lakes, or when I hunt or hike in the woods, or in matters of which I outwardly converse with myself wherever I happen to be, have cumulatively snowballed toward graduated levels of spiritual homage in appreciation of this chance to live. As I age, I seem increasingly drawn to spend much of whatever remains of my time by myself but not in the fashion of an outcast, nutcase, or recluse, don't worry about me in those ways. If I ever show up missing for a spell, say I merit one of those Facebook searches complete with a recent photo, know you can count on me showing back up—thus far I always have. Chances are good I am merely stalled by my own volition, consumed by this pending question, "When in life have you felt most alone?" and am taking ample time with my answer, "As often as I can."

(*339 words*)

Question: *Do you have any regrets?*

Nope.
(*1 word*)

Oh, alright, I'll play fair, but first I would urge *Storyworth* to just up and kill this darling. If I were a senior grandpa hoping for a lasting impression to be handed down to future generations, do I really want to venture into my regrets? I doubt to be speaking solely for myself in saying regrets remain off limits—my faults

I will discuss at length, mistakes, sure, many teaching moments that have slapped me silly over the years—all fair play. But regrets? Do I have any? Oh, probably. Would I select this question as part of my published legacy? No, and I do not regret saying so.

(*109 words*)

These are but a handful of what appear to be hundreds of available questions. Having barely tapped the surface, it's a sure bet we'll be back.

February

February 08—Marriage Stories Appendage 5

The countdown to Karen's retirement is in full bloom—twenty-two days to go. During her thirty-four-year career Karen never, and I do mean *never*, took days off frugally so nobody would dare question her lifelong work ethic. Coming down the homestretch, however, talk about a shark smelling blood. Have a look at her self-augmented workweek upcoming:

Monday: Off—A day to wind down after all the Super Bowl hoopla, although our "party" will include only her, me, Audrey, and Beebee.

Tuesday: Off—Forecast calls for chances of intermittent snow showers starting on Monday night and continuing into the early morning hours. Roads might be dicey, why risk it?

Wednesday: 6:00—2:30.

Thursday: 6:00—2:30.

Friday: Off—Personal Day. Lots of time banked up; "Use it or lose it."

When I sat across our living room good-naturedly joking about her two-day bear of an upcoming workweek she coolly shrugged and replied, "So, fire me."

February 12—Super Bowl Observations

The Rigged NFL

The Super Bowl was played last night, an overtime thriller, but before we go there may we take a look at the latest fad claiming NFL football games are somehow being "rigged"? The matter would not otherwise be worth more than a passing chuckle if so many people didn't *believe* it.

I have been watching the NFL since Sam Huff was tackling Jimmy Brown, so a long time; plenty long enough to cite conventional screwups as a major component to the game. Never a game goes by without fans voicing all sorts of telling phraseology: "*The ball was right in your hands!*" Or, "*Who the hell were you throwing that to?*" Or, "*Why are you passing the ball from the one-yard-line, ya wingnuts?*" And on it goes, and on it shall continue. Dropped passes, inexplicable throws, fumbled footballs, lousy play calling, terrible officiating, missed blocks, missed tackles, and every fuckup imaginable has befallen coaches, players, and refs, since day one and will persist befalling them until a final whistle ever blows. In a game emphasizing rapidity, where a snap of the ball ignites twenty-two players bursting at once, anyone trying to sell mistakes as coerced acts leading to a pre-determined outcome, are simply rationalizing their own failings at what has become the fastest evolving component of *all* of sport, not just the NFL—gambling.

Yes, there has always been gambling, agreed, but today's version, supersized, encouraged, and intensely advertised, permeates straight to an entire population, aggressively bombarding televisions, iPads, laptops, iPhones, and what have you. Marketing "Sports Betting" is a booming commodity, despite the C.Y.A. small print with the phone number to call if you sense you have a "gambling problem." Hint—if you believe the reason you lose bets is due to the NFL being rigged or scripted, yes, for krisesakes, you *do* have a gambling problem. Whenever a gambler's wagers fall short, there are always reliable and observable explanations, all which exclude, "It's rigged."

Nevertheless, by modern standards should a player's mistake cost their team a game, or should a coaching decision backfire, or should a ref make an inept call, and should one or any combination of these screwups juxtapose unfavorably, it is popular provocation for damaged gamblers to howl about the NFL obviously being cheaters.

Queston: If it is true that the NFL's underhandedness lies so vividly bared for all the world to see, wouldn't only the dumbest of all the world's shits be standing in line to place more wagers?

One thing you can consider a sure bet is that gambling was never intended to entice wise folks.

Just to play along, though, imagine the phenomenal cooperation of thirty-two organizations, each formed with invested owners, front office management, coaches, players, and other personnel, and then bring into the mix the one-hundred and twenty-one employed officials along with their higherups, all together working to covertly choreograph a rigged NFL. And even if one could be swayed to believe such a scheme is in play, the next thing to explain is the extraordinary acting. Given how precisely these NFL scripts must unfold at breakneck speed all while synchronizing intricate timing and precision of players and officials racing about and never missing their marks on a stage measuring a hundred yards long by fifty wide is nothing short of astounding! The special effects and circuslike stunts on darned near every play utterly dwarfs even the best versions of reality TV.

Take last night as the world convened to watch this year's Super Bowl. Afterward, Chiefs fans celebrated, Niners fans mourned, and multitudes of gamblers cried foul—did you see how so and so did such and such? It's all rigged.

But the best evidence denying assertions of the NFL being rigged was vividly extracted from the players and coaches immediately following Kansas City's fake overtime win. While it might be easy to embellish jubilance, you must agree the Chief's actors made it look decidedly authentic, hoisting that trophy while feigning credible tears of joy. Academy Awards all around! But if Kansas City's acting seemed unparalleled, look into the eyes and faces of San Francisco's actors after their supposed willingness to fake coming so close for the third time in eleven years, only to fall short once again in another heartbreaker. The resilient adage—*agony of defeat*—surely looked legitimate to clear thinking fans.

If, though, you are one who marginalizes professional sports to suit your own excuses, shortchanging the authenticity of NFL players who break their asses and play their hearts out rising to the pinnacle of their profession, or NFL coaches who have demonstrably proven their worth after years and years prowling the sidelines, or NFL officials who are asked to navigate an increasingly muddied and convoluted sea of everchanging and additional rules being piled onto them, maybe instead of continuously unraveling at the seams every time you lose a bet, you go ahead and call that number at the bottom of your screen.

February 14—Facebook Observations

The very notion the NFL could be rigged indicates how the world we are living in grows progressively tougher on critical thinkers. It becomes a legitimate question, then, how a person who so readily recognizes this erosion could remain so quick to double-click his Facebook page throughout a day... every day. In my defense, I'll try it this way; if all that is left for critical thinkers to do is to ease back and enjoy the show, why not relent and embrace it?

Here is why Facebook takes a toll on critical thinkers, and yes I know this will seem personal, needy, and egotistical, whatever, but bear with me, we are all probably as guilty.

You already know I self-publish books because you are reading one. Each time I publish, I introduce my new work on Facebook where it is welcomed by a handful of friends who "like" my post, along with a few congratulatory comments.

I also, on occasion, have articles professionally published in national magazines. These days my articles are directed solely toward *Deer & Deer Hunting Magazine*, but over the years I have appeared in a gamut of others. The magazine articles somehow seem to draw more "likes" than do the books, along with a few nice comments.

Moving up to the next tier, I routinely post "food" pictures. Karen and I are culinary freaks and show our own food creations, not the clipped-out versions of professionally advertised dishes. Additionally, I generally include short blurbs and careful captioning in describing how we prepare whatever meal or entrée it is I am showing. These food pics garner double the likes and comments than do self-published books and nationally published magazine articles... combined... whatever that says, so you see where this is headed.

To reach the next level of Facebook respondents, this by far the most prolific, I frequently present pictures of hound Audrey and me out in nature—always adorned with loving captioning. At this same stage, I often post pics of hefty fish from glimmering lakes and lastly included here are abbreviated Marriage Stories condensed from the fuller versions you read in these books. If I am at all on my game, this echelon is often lofty enough to amass "likes," "loves," and "laughs," sometimes nearing, or even eclipsing, a forty-count and that's not even including all the esteemed comments.

Now, call me fragile if you wish, it's true, but as much as I want to seem heartened by receiving love from forty or more friends all at one time, I am twice as prone to wondering about the remaining two-hundred and sixty-some no shows. WTF—right?

I'm mostly joking, but if you *really* want to study the overall mindset of social media, I believe I can slam-dunk it.

Earlier this month I must have been frying fish or venison burgers, something like that, from which I emerged from our kitchen bellyaching about grease and oil splattered all over me. Later that week Karen came home from work one evening and took special interest in a package which had arrived during the day. Having no interest myself, I innocently returned to a book I was reading while she tore away at the package. Next thing I knew she stood out in our living room doubled over in laughter.

"Jeepers, Karen," I said, chuckling along, "What's so outrageously funny?"

"This is," she said, and bequeathed to me the contents of her package, "Here ya go, chef of mine."

What she handed to me is a prestigious black plastic kitchen apron boldly scribed with white print below a corny logo of two crossed cleavers and a bunch of flames: *"Shut Up And Eat My Meat."*

Yeah, so, she's a clown.

Well, first things first, this new gift must be posted right away to Facebook. I donned the apron, tied it, and struck a pose at our stovetop while brandishing tongs and a spatula for good staging. Karen fought through her childish giggling to get the shot of me childishly posing, and after she got the right shot I dutifully hastened to get it posted for all to see. In rapid fire, then, from a world where self-published books and nationally acclaimed magazine articles go mostly wasted, where sentimental pics of man and dog, man and wife, and man and dinner, fare only mildly better, an apron reading, *Eat My Meat* suffers no such sloughing. By the time it was over, my new apron had drawn over a hundred hysterical responses and unstoppable comments, none remotely resembling critical thought.

So, you see what I am saying.

February 15—Songs For Springers

I held off mentioning during my Facebook bloodletting, a detached sub-bracket of posts reserved for early morning where I periodically roust a reliable target of early birds, or "springers" as we call ourselves. Count on these posts to be spawned at the hands of some song, or lyrics, which earn elaboration. Those posts are far too poetic for the general Facebook masses so by mid-morning I will have likely taken them down in favor of a picture of my hound or breakfast. The posts, though, are never relegated to oblivion, and it is not at all unusual for some to progress to a more sophisticated audience.

Case in point:

Angels That Promise The Stars

Angels That Promise The Stars is a song recorded by an obscure personal favorite, Miss Leslie (Leslie Anne Sloan) written by her sister, Hilary Sloan. I happened across the song on iTunes during the wee hours not long ago while previewing some of her new material. The song was among several I downloaded, and right away I began playing them back. When *Angels That Promise The Stars* came up I was ripe for the pleasant ambush lurking in the chorus where the line, "*Oh, love, you never warn me about the places where I don't belong,*" leveled its crosshairs. If ever a line could rip through decades and pry an old man from his couch to be tossed back into the fires of bawdy youth, I'm going with that one. And the words don't lie—warning labels rarely adorned our recklessness.

From this exonerative distance, I can claim how my own version of angels promising the stars, against whatever odds, washed out favorably. Judge if you must but I am eternally glad I didn't toe the mark back during the times when everything was still up for grabs and so easy to reach.

Highways and signs give no peace of mind
For knowing the right way to go
Barrooms and questions keep dancin' around
The feelings and what they might show.

Weekend nights, blaring neon lights, ass-kickin' bands—barhopping is what we called it; do they still? All the girls loosening their wraps and dropping their guard as the night wore on, us guys rockin' our cowboy hats and leather boots, reins so loosened that, even if we *were* warned, we would have plowed ahead to places we didn't belong. Our saving grace, like all before us and those to come, is we never caught onto the brevity—how fast our time was burning. Youth is the very heart of the human fire but rages the quickest. How fortunate it turns out, those hottest of embers everlastingly glow.

From the instant I heard the song, and each time since, my old eyes stand guard over the easiest smile on earth while the lyrical masterpiece reawakens three-minutes from my own run at youth so long, long, ago. And after all these years, many of the places where I probably didn't belong nevertheless have left smiles still standing, laughter still echoing, tears long dried, and most of all, memories still glowing.

These days, yes, I'm a balding heap, hearing aids, gout, blood-pressure meds, dentures, knee replacement, and permanent scars from radiation and chemotherapy. But inwardly I cling to a different story. I may be the only one left who can still see him, I get that, but the tough guy of my youth is there alright, still kickin' it up, even as I readily agree, at this age, to adhere to the places where I *do* belong.

But he *is* still there.

March

March 01—That's A Wrap

This morning a new employee will enter through the front doors of Guthrie Medical for the first time; nervous, anxious, excited, and of course with no awareness that over on the other side of the building an icon of yesteryear's workforce will quietly be heading out. Today, when Karen closes the door behind her, she will carry with her a fulfilled commitment, her integrity and work ethic unblemished since walking through the entrance thirty-four years ago.

What would be her first inclination as a new retiree?

That's easy.

Her first steps of retirement, even if only metaphorical, would be to rush back to the front of the building, grab that new employee by the shirttails, and impart upon them the living proof of something well worth striving for. She would next solidify her purpose by allowing them a deliberate and direct look into the eyes of an old soldier—a gift then handed down.

But in real time she will shrug and say, "All I did was go to work each day," as if it's no big deal; but yes, it *is* a big deal. She, by simply upholding a promise to herself, to her employer, and to others of us counting on her, has fulfilled a level of commitment rarely seen these days. Her phenomenal lifelong career in a workforce that didn't always make it easy—especially toward the end, was a grand display of perseverance rarely to be duplicated. I am eager to embrace her joining me in retirement where the only troubles of the day are settling upon Applebee's or Texas Roadhouse, Walmart or Sam's, what day to head for Oak Hill Bulk Foods, and whose turn it is to take Audrey out to pee. Things along that order.

March 04—Blue-collar Versus Office Workers

(Editing Note: Writing blue-collar stories necessitates blue-collar language. Are we good?)

With Karen's working days, along with mine, now in the books, it presents a timely aperture from which to review our polar livelihoods. We nurtured separate niches, hers clerical, mine blue-collar, in teaming up to climb our mutual ladder. Our occupational livelihoods were of utmost importance to each of us and especially to each other. We stayed earnest in fulfilling our commitments to hold down jobs to fortify our marriage.

I can't feign any authority about the clerical/office side of the coin except to say I saw enough through the cracks over the years to reinforce my contentment of having stayed in my blue-collar lane.

And let's be honest, whatever Karen saw over those same years kept her preferring I stay outdoors, too.

You remember Nate, my younger friend, who for several years back in his college days worked as an employee of mine. What Nate likes to do lately is send me Facebook "reels" as they are called, or Instagram videos, featuring construction bosses throwing what appear to be profane tirades but are in real time mostly staged reenactments intended for clowning. It is evident that Nate still holds dear to his heart some of the old flareups he witnessed, many of those closeup. For my part, I laugh along as a good sport. Let me show you the latest one he sent.

To begin the video, we see the boss leaping down from his backhoe where he can more intently address his crew of four or five guys doing the handwork down in the trenches of what looks to be the makings of some sort of foundation under way. Perched above the trench, the rugged and weathered old boss, ball hat, blue jeans, scuffed up boots, you know the look, narrows his eyes on a particular worker and demands, quote: "Gimme that tape-measure." The worker, as directed, lobs the tape-measure up from the trench. The boss snags the tape from midair and in the same motion wheels and side arms it off to no man's land with the intensity of a major league infielder firing a ball to nip a speedy baserunner. Of course, an uprising of comical laughter ensues as his crew follows the tape-measure soaring to its demise. Because I can fully relate, staged or not, let me assure you the laughter is something the boss wryly intended. With the tape-measure bouncing discordantly to its death in the site's residual dirt, the boss glares back at the trench and growls, "If ya don't know how to read a goddamned tape-measure could ya at least try to keep up shovelin'?" The crew had by now turned so predictably delirious that unknowing outsiders might think them to have witnessed the greatest show on earth. But, no, it is merely a common scene played out every single day coast to coast, just the ongoing blue-collar backbone of how the toughest work gets done across our land.

As implied, I learned early on the only place for me was with blue-collars. I fit in immediately, loved the verbal leniencies, thrived upon the jocular banter, marveled at how fluently any disagreements or arguments were resolved by day's end, and most of all thoroughly embraced how creating laughter, either inspiring it or causing it, was a badge of honor. The admiration and communal respect which hard workers keep front and center toward one another results in an eternally ingrained camaraderie. I am, to this day, happily bound to an everlasting kinship with the hard workers of this country.

Back to Nate's incessant baiting, I knew not to expect world peace when he served up my favorite of all, this one titled: *Blue-collar Guy Applies For Office Job*. The short, staged, video opens with our blue-collar hopeful misplaced in an office setting, dressed innocently in his hard-hat, jeans, boots, and a tattered sweatshirt. You only get one chance at a first impression, so giving it his all he blurts to a third party off screen, "What's up, motherfucker, you must be the *big* boss, huh?"

Right away, though, the "big boss," obviously HR, draws back aghast.

"There is *no cussing* in this building!"

"Oh, jeepers, yeah, sorry," says the blue-collar guy, cumbersomely, "I won't say that again."

Surely, I needn't go frame by frame. The interview blows up, a predictable train wreck, the disillusioned blue-collar guy habitually does, repeatedly in fact, say that again and again until failing the interview so badly he coarsely throws in the towel: "Fuck this, fuck you, and fuck this office shit. I'm goin' back out with my boys. This is bullshit."

These staged versions are exaggerated, anyone can see that, but not as grossly as one might imagine. Explore with me the comment section of this video for a more detailed appraisal.

Aaron: "I thrive on going to work and spending twelve hours a day getting paid to flip my coworkers off when I walk or drive past them."

Derek: "If I didn't get flipped off by my fellow forklift operators, I would think they were mad at me."

Autumn: "My dad and brothers could never work in an office setting; they've always worked blue-collar. I work in an ER where the staff are very similar. They're an HR nightmare. ER staff are brutal, vulgar, and abrasive. They're my favorite kind of people to work with."

Josh: "How do you make it through twelve-hour days without talking shit? Sounds miserable."

Doug: "Tried office work once. HR had a meeting with me where she suggested 'sensitivity training.' Without skipping a beat I said, 'Yeah, sure, not a problem. Send in the whole bunch.' At Christmas time I asked her if she got me a gift. We saw so much of each other I was tempted to get her one."

Max piggybacked: "Lol, Doug. I have to know, are you now married to the HR lady, and do you still work there?"

Eric: "I worked in an office for a long time. The environment is way different, the biggest difference is the strange culture of trust and respect in construction. Probably a lot of brain damage and alcoholism to thank for that, haha."

Wilko: "True. In blue-collar there is an honesty between the blokes which does not exist in white collar spaces."

Rebecca: "I went from construction to office. I miss construction, especially taking home all the scrap materials and demo hardware... but here I get to wear my comfies and bring my dog to work, so..."

Julian (Choosing a diplomatic approach): "Blue-collar is like the cool side of the family; office is more like the classy side."

But, face it, diplomacy doesn't enjoy any wiggle room with this bunch.

Gabriel: "I'd like to see this video made with a roofer instead of a regular construction worker."

Jacob: "So in Spanish?"

Jeffrey: "Not much difference except roofers have to miss work once a month to talk to their parole officer."

Alright, enough, but my god, I could laugh like this all day long. We need to move along so let's ask Ian to wind this down.

Ian: "Yeah, I don't think I'd do very good at a fuckin' office job."

No, probably not, Ian; probably not.

Because I spent my entire working career with these people, I know I can trust you to appreciate how badly at times I do miss it. With some reluctance, then, I will close out this entry but ask you to indulge my favorite story, one I never tire of.

I once hired a new employee who took no time at all in evaluating, to everyone's delight, especially mine, my small potential for office work. Our days were tough enough so that sometimes new workers needed extra coaching to help keep them in the game. On this employee's second morning I was staying tight as a teen's skirt to him, hoping to be mixing in a healthy dose of jocular humor to offset some of my admittedly unrefined means of motivation. Apparently "jocular humor" is a subjective term which previously unbeknown to me comes with parameters. Who knew? I am unsure of what all I must have said—I never really cared, but along came our ten o'clock break, one I shall always remember. Amid our conventional breaktime banter this new employee glanced up from his lunchpail, steadied his focus directly at me, and as straightforwardly as I believe it can be done, flatly stated, "Kriste, you'd be hauled to HR before lunchtime on your first day at a regular fuckin' job."

Agreed.

March 07—Marriage Stories Appendage 6

Her retirement has begun, so even as I slept in until 6:00, exuberantly exhausted from a brutal, all-day, soaking rain yesterday on Keuka Lake where I piled up a good catch of perch, Karen remained soundly sleeping. By the time she finally toddled out, yawning, and groggily making her way toward the coffee, I had long since gained high gear. Frankly, I think it surprises her to see such practiced fluency going on around here, something she hasn't yet had much chance to directly observe. During my working years I navigated the outdoors like a champ, it's how I made my living, so no surprises there; but since my own retirement a couple years ago, Karen has not been home to witness my indoor transformation. For the past couple of years, each day upon her return from work, Karen has walked into a pristine setting, folded blankets on our couch, vacuumed flooring, dusted shelving, sparkling mirrors and glasswork, rarely a dirty dish, laundry magically hanging back in the closets, and more often than not dinner is either underway or shortly will be. But only now that she is officially retired is she beholding firsthand—this... this... this *miracle*.

On the morning I want to tell you about, like I said, I had sprung from the couch after crash-landing there for the night. Right away I started brewing coffee and got busy rounding up my sodden clothes from yesterday, some I had stripped off down in the basement, some still out in the truck, all to be corralled and loaded into the washer. Back upstairs, I poured coffee and opened the fridge to retrieve the perch fillets from my Tuesday's catch, filleted Wednesday morning, and left to firm up overnight in the fridge, and now ready for packaging for the freezer—a familiar process. With that task completed I gathered a second load of laundry and trod back down to the basement where I paused to stash the perch fillets into the freezer before continuing over to the washer and dryer to rotate my laundry. As long as I was down there, I tended Beebee's litter box.

(At this point Karen is still sound asleep, a relevancy I mention casually, but please note it is now past 7:00.)

From Beebee's litter box, I swung over near the work benches to collect yesterday's catch of perch to take upstairs and get them filleted and refrigerated, a procedure consuming most of the next hour. Fish cleaning is a noisy event, lots of clanging and banging against the stainless-steel sink, high-pitched electric knife slicing through bone, the thumping of spoil tossed into the plastic bucket, nobody could sleep through it. So, for those keeping score Karen finally made her dreary-eyed debut sometime around 7:45, probably closer to 8:00—mid-morning as I like to call it. She graced her entrance managing a forced smile, mumbled an insipid "g'morning," poured coffee, and sleepily retreated to the living room to plop in her spot on the couch and nurse her newfound snail's pace at waking.

I remained in the kitchen to finish up my perch and then needed to haul the spoil bucket out to the woods—may as well take Audrey along so she can cover her morning rituals. We did that, and back inside I rinsed my spoil bucket before whipping Auddie up a hearty hound's breakfast of high-quality kibble mixed with a generous handful of shredded chicken breast. I tossed a smaller portion of chicken to Beebee on my way to the sink where I quickly knocked out what few dishes could be handwashed. I placed the rest of the dishes, the ones I don't handwash, into the dishwasher.

By now the laundry downstairs could be leapfrogged but before tending that I headed outside to my boat to plug in the battery charger and top off the gas.

My proficient whirlwind of resourceful nonstop activity deserving an intermission, I returned upstairs, poured a cup of coffee, and joined Karen in the living room. I guessed she might be alert enough for moderate conversation, but she seemed engrossed in her iPhone so I left her to it while silently checking my own iPhone to see what new riveting Facebook posts might await. After only a brief interlude, however, I swear I heard her say to me, "Did you take your pills?"

... Let's review.

Even having slept in myself, meaning until 6:00 AM, I nonetheless jumped into action checking boxes left 'n right, accomplishing more in two hours than most people do before noon, all of this against the backdrop of my wife slumbering in her retirement, which of course I have no argument against; let her sleep, she's earned it. But what I want to know, or *need* to know, is if it is accidental, or is it on purpose, how she could so cooly negate my torrid pace of productivity in favor of homing in on the one lousy thing I missed doing during my sunrise crusade.

Before you answer, let me additionally point out that "my pills" entail a vitamin E gel, a tiny baby aspirin, a half-pill to guard against gout, and lastly, a dinky pink pill I don't even think I need for blood pressure. In other words, lest I project an air of detached indifference, who cares?

But what fun is that?

To address her inquiry, I deliberately worked up my best deadpan face and flatly lied, "No, I did not take my pills. And given our new living arrangement of you being here twenty-four-seven, you might as well know I've been flushing those things down the toilet for years."

She cast an affectionate eyeroll, smiled sweetly, and returned to her podcast.

Footnote—Round Two.

(*A few weeks later...*):

When I am not, quote: "Running around the house like a madman," in the mornings, it is common for us, during the first hour or so, to roost silently in our living room on separate corners of twin couches. "Quiet Time," is what she calls it. During Quiet Time, I tend to read or else retreat to my headphones and listen to music while Karen is more apt to tune into one of her chosen podcasts. This morning when I broke the silence by announcing, "I need to get something out to thaw for dinner," and asked Kare if she had any requests, she replied, "No, whatever you want is okay with me."

I went to the kitchen where I refilled my coffee and noticed, next to the sink, the two emptied plastic chicken liver jars I had left soaking in soap and water overnight (I use chicken livers for bullhead bait.) I finished cleaning the containers and dried them, ready now to store down in the basement where they may eventually come in handy for... I don't know... something. As long as I was going downstairs I grabbed a clothes basket, loaded it with laundry, and took it along. Laundry going, I stowed my liver jars for future use, unplugged my boot dryer, disconnected the charger to my night light, and, of course, tended Beebee's litter box. There. Great. I returned upstairs, grabbed my coffee refill, and toted it back to the living room where I rejoined Karen.

"So," she began innocently, "What did you end up getting out for dinner, Chef Rog?"

So that's how that went...

March 18—Marriage Stories Appendage 7

Lights Fights

I have probably covered this, but to be sure let me reiterate my having purposely installed dimmer switches on all our interior lighting, and reiterate as well, Karen's prominent dismissal. Karen approaches light switches in a manner of either/or, with the kicker that all lights are to be left on throughout the day until nightfall whereupon all lights are totally terminated. In other words, Karen unconditionally rejects the conceptual advantages of dimmer switches. I suppose one could call me equally rigid in the way I go about extinguishing lights which are not in use, so it's even-steven in some respects. But on this I am firm; there is nothing fair about how she walks around here walloping these dimmer switches. Fairness regarding dimmer switches is plain as day, at least as I see it. The objective is to obtain a desired ambience, so tell me what could be more straightforward than to simply mirror daylight? Early in the morning start out with a slow tempering glow emulative of a soothing sunrise. As the day hits its stride approaching noontime and throughout the afternoon hours, go ahead and jack the things, who cares. Finally, toward the receding end of the day, dampen the lighting accordingly settling for a comforting luminosity leading quietly to bedtime, when, and only when, everything goes black. What could possibly be flawed about a well-conceived plan to utilize the assuasive rationale of harmonious lighting so fully?

Ah, I might be playing it up a bit, we have things well enough ironed out to avoid fisticuffs and to be fair, myself, she never argues when I walk about adjusting the lighting... well, almost never... there was this one.

We had recently finished eating in the living room and Karen, as she usually does, kindheartedly picked up my dinner plate and silverware on her way back to the kitchen. I rarely blacken the kitchen lights knowing how regimented we are at coming right back, the kitchen has loosened rules, but nobody's perfect. Karen, finding the kitchen as black as Steinbeck's "eye of despair" needed to juggle some silverware before she could activate the twin light switches. Her transfer went amiss, she fumbled a handful of silverware careening across our laminate flooring. Her slipup, at least to me, wasn't worth more than a light chuckle until she let fly this gem: "Thanks a lot Mister Lights Out. Could we *possibly* act any more like old people?"

Honestly, I marvel at how seamlessly that girl can allocate fault elsewhere. I hope that doesn't sound abrasive. The truth is I willingly absorb her niftiness, it is always funny, but even better regarding this particular flub wherein, if I heard correctly, she seemed to deny that we are old yet.

To fully complete the story, (why am I even mentioning this) you can bet those kitchen lights stayed burning on full-beam upon her return to the living room.

March 21—Happy Birthday, Audrey Girl

Karen and I have housed hounds for most of our lives, and I have said before how they have cumulated to show us better sides of ourselves.

Today we commemorate Audrey's twelfth birthday, and I want to say something out loud specifically about her. Auddie's predecessors, Tina and Daisy, romped with me during seasons of my youth, our hiking routine rarely interrupted, I was simply always there. But Audrey and I have ridden a bit of a rollercoaster. I vividly remember, and always will, during my cancer treatments, tearfully moving to her side in the middle of one of those darkest nights to pet her and tell her none of this was her fault. It was a gesture mostly for my own good, I get that, but I somehow felt compelled, anyhow, to tell her. It is a bad memory, but an important one. After cancer, we rallied until my knee faltered whereupon we were again sidelined for a time. Once my knee healed, we were back on track, when out of the blue Audrey wound up needing a toe amputated. I know I'm droning, but the good news is we are both at last healthy and back on top of things. I don't think she needs to hear this, but I need to say it. The hikes we are taking these days, fleeting as we both know they are, and nowhere rivaling the distance or intensity of those on which I embarked with Tina and Daisy, are nonetheless the most exhilarating of my life. I am positive the other dogs would not feel shorted by my feeling this way. The distinguishing circumstances between Audrey and me, periodically helping each other back up off the ground from the hurdles we have each been summoned to contend, have brought forth the purest angle from where to view hounds and their owners showing each other the very best sides of themselves.

    Happy Birthday, little friend... and thank you.

April

April 01—April Fools' Day

I am currently midway through a book titled, *Canary In A Covid World*, which will merit expansion upon completion. It is a compilation of thirty-four substantially credentialed, patently honest, and uncontestably courageous contributors. In lieu of April Fools' Day, I want to isolate a term in which these authors are routinely confronted in an intentional attempt to keep them silenced. Thankfully the effort is failing, which is good for us all. The term is "disinformation" (deliberately misleading), not to be confused with misinformation—unintentionally misleading.

The original principle of disinformation is linked to military strategy—intentional sleight of hand to tactically mislead opponents to focus away from the main attack. Great in military application, but not so great in the hands of politically motivated opportunists, especially when so many Americans obediently fall in line.

Here is how bad it gets. Watch how the group, *American Psychological Association,* selectively deploys deliberate disinformation regarding... disinformation.

"The spread of disinformation has affected our ability to improve public health, address climate change, maintain a stable democracy, and more. By providing valuable insight into how and why we are likely to believe disinformation, psychological science can inform how we protect ourselves against its ill effects."

Plainly and brashly, *American Psychological Association* grants themselves permission to decide for us all what constitutes disinformation, and in doing so, declares themselves to be the trusted sole arbitrators of what must therefore constitute legitimate information. Step two for them is to flunk any competing information as obvious disinformation. How convenient! Climate change? Public Health? Stable Democracy? Well, hold on a sec. A lot of exceptional minds contend that climate change, public health, and "stable" democracy, are not one-sided or closed issues. Why would a free-thinking society allow voices from exceptional minds to be suppressed? Any society persuaded to forfeit disagreement as evidence of disinformation is a controlled society, politically contaminated. Meaningful conversations intended to advance intelligent approaches of handling essential issues are of no interest to the politically contaminated. That is not how they operate. *American Psychological Association* makes it clear how the politically contaminated maneuver by their preposterous gall to use the term, "psychological science." Psychological science describes unabated propaganda—precisely how the military uses disinformation.

I wish this example of unchecked belligerence were confined to the field of psychology, but the advent of "fact checkers" is an in-your-face invasion launched from powerful entities with the collective ability to restrain our societal freedom to their liking. The attempt to seize ownership and distribution of information is happening every day and right in front of our eyes under the guise of "fact checkers," a would-be benevolent assemblage to protect us from lies and deceit. But clear thinking people unveil "fact checkers" as *propagating* disinformation. Clear thinking people distinguish "fact checker" as, not a person, but an orchestrated entity of politicized strongarming. Clear thinking people know it is a fact that "fact checkers" perpetually and strategically lie.

For those who continue to insist on falling for such charades, this day is for you—Happy April Fools' Day.

April 06—Stories That Write Themselves

Jan Billings was a high school English teacher who enjoyed a long and fruitful career. Back in the early seventies when I knew her, she was Miss Antenucci until one day we students plopped into our seats to be ecstatically ambushed by her announcement that she and another of our favorite English teachers, Mr. (Ross) Billings, were now as one. I was a student of each, taking their classes throughout my high school years, classes conducted by mentors who motivated, encouraged, and propelled my love for words.

Recently, out of the blue, I received a group email announcing a high school reunion of sorts, inviting all alumni who attended Magnolia High School during the 1970's. Magnolia High School is located in Southern California, and I have reconnected with a few of the old gang via Facebook, but when it comes to anything reunion themed, I'm out. How my name is still included in any guest list is a mystery, but I opened it anyhow, caving to the teaser, "Look Who's Coming!" I recognized a handful of student names but when teachers were listed, I recognized them all, particularly Jan Billings. The chance to contact her, if only to say how every facet of my lifetime has been enhanced by literary doings, was not something to let pass so I typed out a brief reply to the email.

Hi Tim, (the organizer.)

Thanks for the email. I noticed in the list of teachers who will be attending, Jan Billings. There is so much I would like to say to her if you will be good enough to relay this much. I am not sure if Ross is still with us, but the two of them were gigantically instrumental in my writing career. I am far short of a household name, but I am routinely published nationally in numbers of outdoor magazines and have authored a dozen self-published books. I won't belabor here, but if you would pass my email address to her and ask that she contact me, I would be grateful. I will hope for her to see this, and know she will appreciate a quote from the "Acknowledgements" in my first book in which I thanked numbers of higherups in the outdoor literary world but in the end knew who to thank most... and so I did:

"There is one more acknowledgement of which I fear I am decades late. I still possess a high school yearbook in which my English teacher back then, Mr. Billings, signed off: "Good luck Roger—Keep on writin'." Although it took me a while, Mr. Billings, I am finally living up to what you must have seen in me nearly a lifetime ago. I should probably thank you most of all."

Thanks, Tim. I'll trust you to get this to her. I appreciate it.

Roger

Tim promptly replied, thanking me and assuring me he had forwarded my thoughts onward to Jan.

A few hours later my eyes widened anxiously upon receiving her reply.

Dear Roger,

I am so happy to hear you are still "writin'"! And, before I go any further, I would love whatever information you can send me so I can read what you have written.

Sadly, we lost Ross in 2022. He was a modern "Renaissance" man in ways few really know: artist, inventor, builder, designer, filmmaker etc., and much of this ahead of his time. Importantly, he was a devoted family man. We now have 13 grandchildren and 13 great grandchildren - quite a legacy. Your acknowledgment is heartwarming, and I know he is grateful for your sentiments. He did, indeed, see something in you that you, yourself, perhaps did not fully acknowledge.

Quick and relevant story: Growing up in Sioux Falls, SD, his parents were loving but not well-versed on opportunities for their son. College and careers were not discussed. He shared with me that in his sophomore English class one day, he experienced a life-changing moment. It was not overtly dramatic, but it was profound. Without it, you would not have met him or experienced time with him. His teacher, a young but sensitive and insightful young man, was strolling among the class as they were writing essays. He stopped by Ross's desk, looked down at his essay, put his hand on Ross's shoulder and whispered, "Ross, this is very very good! Very good! Keep going." And that was it. In that moment, his future was born. It took him 9 years while working full time, to get his credential. As teachers, we never know how we might impact students. With your email, Roger, he and we know. It is a gift. Thank you.

Please let me know where I can find your writing. Looking forward to your next email,

Jan

Her story about Ross having been propelled so intensely from the encouragement of his own teacher, sent me unashamedly into an instantaneous emotional meltdown, as it struck dead center into the heart of my own devotion toward mentorship and how significantly important it is for mentors to full-heartedly pass to those in our footsteps anything at all we feel might lighten their paths. It is a gift both ways, and when Jan thought enough of me to share that story as one of "relevancy," my eyes let loose, and I needed some time for that.

I replied right away but only enough to thank her for getting back to me while asking her to give me some time so I could answer more properly. It took me a day or two but given my chance to thank her personally I chose my words with great care.

Thanks for giving me some time with this, Jan. I wound up nearly overwhelmed to receive your email. Your touching tribute to Ross is exactly how my wife and I feel toward one another and it is so good to see. We have no children so I did chuckle at your current roll call of twenty-six and can envision a pretty unruly classroom at times. I will send you a few books and ask you to read them sequentially to cover most anything I would otherwise detail about the lifetime between here and high school, but I will take this opportunity to say thank you in a more personal sense.

You would have little way of knowing my home situation which direly lacked paternal guidance. I was lucky to have a wise and weathered mother who guided me toward football coaches for the tougher stuff, but with equal enthusiasm she championed what she saw as an evolving aptitude for words. Whether or not she was personally aware of my teachers by name, she certainly realized that beneath my rougher veneer I was nurturing a deep-seated respect toward them and that made her happy, even proud. To whomever these teachers were who were cultivating this kid's drive to type out stories and essays, my mother stayed quietly indebted. She is the one who insisted in eighth grade that I learn typing. I bitched and moaned, of course, "typin' ain't cool," but it turned out to be a favorite class in which I wound up the perpetual runner-up during our "timed writings" to some girl in there who could burn the blazes out of that keyboard. I must have never beat her because if I had it would have merited a ticker-tape parade. Anyhow, as I entered high school, my mother presented me with an ultimate luxury, are you ready... an electric typewriter—ELECTRIC!! I would dare not tell that story to many these days, but I bet you understand. So, my road to you and Ross was somewhat paved by external influences, too. I had a lot of English teachers encourage me along my way, but for whatever reasons you and Ross stand out as, "Without them... who knows?"

I am confident you will notice throughout my writing that my respect and homage toward mentorship and learning hasn't waned. I have now mentored my share of kids throughout my livelihood as a landscape contractor and trust you to smile knowingly as being a part of that ongoing process. Teaching and learning are the two most formidable components to fulfillment, and I shall always treasure my good luck in crossing paths with you and Ross among the others who showed it to me.

If you will provide a mailing address I want to send you three books. I have authored several, but many are topic-specific, so the three I have chosen are aimed at general audiences. You are of course welcome to any of the others you want, just say the word. You can see them all at Amazon.

If you read the books in chronological order it will offer the clearest procession of a person you helped make. (This I say excluding some of the language and political flareups you will occasionally run across—you didn't do that—he laughs—tentatively.)

Thank you so much, Jan, for getting back with me. It is beyond gratifying to be able to thank you personally for the remarkable influence you provided during my formative years.

Yours,
Roger

She supplied an address, and I went ahead and mailed the books from the distance of over fifty years. Along with the package went my high hopes for Jan to gain a firsthand glimpse of the fruits of her and Ross's labor. Sure, my self-published work is nothing big league, either are a few semesters in a classroom. But when the highlights of a lifetime can stay traced back to those classrooms in such a way that an English teacher is sitting down to books authored by her student, both parties might bask in what can only be perceived as a league of their own.

Two days after mailing the books, Karen and I sat down to breakfast with my brother Ron and his wife Cheryl at a favorite diner up their way. Shortly into the conversation I revealed the exciting news about making contact with Jan when Cheryl stunned me with something I hadn't considered.

"She *remembered* you?" asked Cheryl.

I felt my face fall momentarily blank before stammering, "Uh, ya know... I don't know. I *think* she did, her email seemed to carry a personal tone but..." and my voice trailed off to an awkward silence until I shrugged and chuckled, "Heck if I know."

From there the question lingered beyond breakfast until seizing a solid foothold in my mind. Midweek is when I received the next email from Jan acknowledging the safe arrival of the books. She thanked me and promised she would dive right in; "What a treat," is how she signed off.

Desiring an answer to the looming question, I typed back:

Thanks Jan,

Hey, I have to ask, and you can laugh, I would, too, but out to breakfast with my brother and sister-in-law over the weekend I mentioned contacting you after all these years and my sister-in-law tossed this eye-opener out: "And she REMEMBERED you?"

Well, I hadn't thought of that, had I? My bewildered silence was good for a laugh but did bring to light, while it is easy for a student to remember their teachers it is not so easy the other way around. I guess it shouldn't matter much, the general takeaway is for you to know the lasting impact you had on at least one student, whomever this person might be, hahahaha, (and I can surmise hundreds of others.)

I hope you enjoy the reading; nothing brick 'n mortar, but it's a real treat for a writer, too, to be able to construct a book wall-to-wall and call it their own. My lifetime with words has been the greatest payoff of all, so thank you for your pivotal role in that, Jan. Forever appreciated.

Roger.

I sent the email intent on convincing myself that if it turned out Jan had to do some research to find out who this Roger Page person was I would be okay with that. I probably would have been, too, but after reading her response I can openly declare how preferable it feels to know I made my own impact.

Yep! You can tell everyone at the table that yes, indeed, this is the boy I remember and the young writer he was destined to be.

Not many students in our long careers (she is, of course, including Ross) *were spoken about to each other, but when a student loved what we loved, it was special and memorable.*

Let's leave this story told enough for the time being. I am hopeful Jan will comment on the books down the road, but if not, I remain wholly fulfilled from being able to personally thank such a mentor and especially to hear in her own words what she and Ross saw in me all those years ago. Since our time together back in those California classrooms, every written word of mine remains lined with the structural influences and positive encouragement bequeathed from a bevy of English teachers, and at the top of that list are Jan and Ross Billings.

Reiterating—forever appreciated.

April 16—White Rural Rage?

Paul Waldman and Tom Schaller are authors of sorts, too, but par them with artists of the late sixties and early seventies who used to get high on hallucinatory drugs and lob paintballs against easels. How else would a book titled, *White Rural Rage: The Threat To American Democracy*, come about? Any degree of sanity would stand in the way. I have no intention of reading it—some books you *can* judge by the cover, but numerous reviews and a couple of revealing quotes from the authors themselves will more than suffice.

Ultimately, Waldman's and Schaller's poorly camouflaged purpose is to dismantle the Electoral College. They champion formal democracy, majority rule, where population centers garner absolute power. Underestimating an entire segment of society, though, has always proven misguided, (remember "deplorables") and not surprisingly these authors found the tables turned a full one-eighty. The threat to American democracy is real, no argument there, and these authors published a prime example.

The electoral process, wisely constructed by our nation's founders, is the only way to give *all* Americans *equal* representation. The intelligence and foresight of our founders to implement the Electoral College ensures all Americans to have a say in all governing processes. An act of genius, the electoral process is the fulcrum decreeing freedom for all, not just some. Any American opposed should be asked to explain their disparagement of fairness.

Waldman and Schaller, by boorishly miscalculating "angry" "white" and "rural" as easy marks, were delivered a blowback as gargantuan as it was deserved. Summing from the reviews and corroborated by a pitiful book rating, Waldman and Schaller condescendingly assumed a lack of intelligence infested rural whites so badly that they collectively stood as sitting ducks, primed for brainwashing by the dangerous Donald Trump. Such feeble-minded loyalty, claim Waldman and Schaller, centers angered white rural people at the core of threatening America's democracy. The solution is simple: nullify these angry hillbillies by robbing them of their electoral voice.

It is fortunate that a handful of people have indeed purchased and somehow stomached reading the book so they can save us the agony. If you deem me as being unfair, myself, in critiquing a book I haven't read, I won't argue, but I did play fair in selecting the reviews, and there is no denying whatsoever the authors' own words.

First a few reviews and expounding notes, then a pertinent quote from each author. My bet is you, like I, will absolve rural people of posing any threat to American democracy.

(All reviews were found at Amazon)

Chance Meyers

I can assure you they haven't heard our voice and they have unfortunately forgotten how much they are dependent on us. Agriculture thrives here, and it is the backbone of our economy and the world's. Everything in the world always has and always will be tied to our basic necessities. Rural communities grow food, and we do it better every year. There is no greater innovation or technological breakthrough in any other industry. We're not living in the past, and we are not the least bit confused.

Stephen Putman
What a patronizing and demeaning book. The authors admitted, in their interview on MSNBC, that Trump spoke to people in rural areas and told them the TRUTH that the system had let them down. They recognize that fact and then go on to describe rural white people as uneducated, ignorant, racist, xenophobic, and Anti-Gay. You're demonizing an entire group of Americans because you hate Donald Trump.

These are common voices from the rural America Waldman and Schaller mistakenly thought easy to marginalize. Chance and Stephen represent *authentic voices* of rural America where we are quite adept at proceeding logically and cutting to the truth by means of honesty, not strategy; a progression foreign to these authors.

Kelly Almond
I heard the authors interviewed and it sounds like a good book. I look forward to reading before I make a judgment. There is a real division in America between cities and rural. Probably always has been. Jobs and services are hard to come by in rural areas, so they cling to cultural issues. Late-stage capitalism is killing these folks.

Walking Contradiction (No name ascribed)
I actually read this book so others won't be subjected to this pandering of urbanites. I've lived in

both rural and urban areas; the latter currently as I am attending college.

The book goes into depth about cities being the epicenter of culture and that people living in metropolitan areas are oppressed by the people living in rural areas and not just any people, "whites" are behind it all.

From my personal experience it's the major cities that determine State law and policy; we desperately need a State Electoral College, as we're edging closer and closer to "tyranny of the majority" as coined by Alexis De Tocqueville.

The constant crying out for "our" democracy, is getting extremely worn out. What those people are really saying is it's only a democracy if you vote the way they do; not only that, but if you don't you're ignorant (at best) and need to be saved from yourself.

I wouldn't take political advice from someone who writes a book intentionally driving a wedge between people.

Kelly and Walking Contradiction show a telling contrast between people; some mired in stereotyped speculation (Kelly), versus those (WC) who have taken pains to study the truth, convey it accurately, and can be trusted with it.

Kelly's confounded observations land impotently, even humorously. Anyone can tell that he (*his* photo was attached) is as unfamiliar with rural life as the authors are. Bemoaning the supposed plight of rural folks is as goofy as *Hee Haw* reruns. We have *not* been repeatedly bamboozled, we do *not* feel deprived of any rights, and the cultural issues Kelly claims we "cling" to are the very freedoms city populations are *sacrificing*. And if jobs and work are hard to come by, it's news to us. Where I live in upstate New York's spacious and sparsely populated farmland country, aside from one immediate neighbor weaseling his way through disability "benefits," everybody else I know for miles around are either working at, or have retired from, fruitful careers. My wife and I are each retired now but leave behind us a cumulative history surpassing seventy-five years in the work force. Kelly's cute slogan, "late-stage capitalism," exposes *his* vulnerability, not ours. We are not the ones meekly caving to socialism, or "late-stage capitalism," as it's sold. Capitalism is alive and well, Kelly, and rural America will continue trying to save your ass in preserving it, so we should be applauded, not eulogized. The reason this book is rated a solid 1.9 out of 5.0 is due to rural people, white, black, Hispanic, male, female, gay, and whatnot, rejecting the ongoing absurdities currently swallowing our nation's cities whole.

Walking Contradiction, laudably less emotional than I, surgically strips this book bare as a failed exercise of attempted exploitation. WC entirely understands the essence of our Electoral College, even calling for States to get on board. You cannot obtain equal representation in accordance with where the masses congregate. Minus an Electoral College, our country's rural population becomes, essentially, muted.

Anyone fighting to eliminate our country's electoral system is, *by definition*, a threat to America's democracy. Rural folks of *all* skin colors remain solidly aligned, not behind the politics of Donald Trump, but with The Constitution of the United States.

I want to clarify that I find Kelly Almond's assessment innocently erroneous. His perception and sympathy are not in mean spirit, but I do wish Americans would grow more apt at understanding the propagandistic noise we are continuously being fed. In rebutting Kelly, though, never would I accuse him of ill intentions.

Not the same for Edward Westerfield. Westerfield is among the politically contaminated who thrive on ill intentions by striking cynically, blinded to their own senselessness fueled further by buckling in hysteria at the name, Donald Trump.

Edward Westerfield
Look at the avalanche of 1-star reviews.
This book scores a direct hit into the mindset of white christofascist salt of the earth pipo. The invective drips off the reviews. Psychological projection at it's finest.

If you were one of the 30% of rural America who didn't vote for 45, or your some woke librul who doesn't understand how anyone can't see the hitleresque insanity of Trump, this book is for you.

This is an important book. It gives insight into the power of Trump in the remnants of the R party.

I left it unedited. Far be it from me to toy with words like christofascist and librul. The only importance anyhow is to accurately pinpoint invective. There is zero invective derived from multitudes of 1-star ratings; the avalanche of 1-star reviews is not an indicator of rage nor invective, it is a valid response to a failed cheap trick of "psychological projection at its finest." And for the benefit of everyone in Westerfield's camp, you should know that the overwhelming rejection of this "important book" comes in all colors.

From The Authors Themselves

With their own words, Waldman and Schaller will solidly confirm the slanted mentality they somehow thought readers would buy into.

From Tom Schaller:
The excess coronavirus deaths in rural counties should be classified as suicides by scientific skepticism. By rejecting proven vaccines, conspiracy-addled rural Americans, though living in communities where social distancing was easier than in densely populated cities, squandered their geographic advantage.

All told, premature deaths from reduced healthcare access and facility closures, healthcare ignorance and scientific skepticism, and a fatal devotion to guns and drugs are killing rural white Americans—especially downscale rural whites.

No, any attempt to calculate "excess" deaths during the coronavirus are negated by the fact that "causes" of death were so disgustingly lied about in the first place. And if the nonsensical term, "scientific skepticism," means to imply skepticism about science, proper wording reveals skepticism applied to science is *essential*, not suicidal. Skepticism is at the *helm* of science. In the case of coronavirus, "selective" science ran amok and warranted skepticism wall to wall. Now, a few years past the Covid Games, we can reliably declare how off base anyone is who called, or continues to call, Covid "vaccines" "proven." What *is* proven is how emphatically wrong Schaller was about injectable products at the time and evidently still is. As far as social distancing, what geographical advantage exists to six-foot distancing? It's rhetorical, the truth about social distancing was best demonstrated in restaurants where we masked up on our way to our table, sat down and took our masks off—so score another mark on the side of skepticism. Where Schaller really tanks, though, is by revealing his tired tactical insistence that it is our "fatal devotion" to guns and drugs that are wiping out all of us "downscale rural whites."

What if I told you, Tom, you have described, with dead-nuts accuracy, inner-city blacks?

If Schaller seems imbecilic, Waldman wastes less time with this tidy quote:

We are all in this together.

Paul Waldman said that. With a straight face. The same person arguing fervently against the Electoral College while co-penning a book based cover to cover on fabrication and falsification of an entire segment of our country, somehow claims we are *all* in this together? All of us, Paul? Don't you mean except anyone living outside the population centers, especially angry whites? There are a lot of people living in rural America, white, black, brown, or otherwise, and we are *not* in this. Most of all, we are not a threat to America's democracy, but a rather significant threat to those who threaten us first. Lucky for you guys, we aren't exactly shaking in our boots over your limp-dick 1.9 rating.

April 27—The Actual Threat To Our Democracy

I promise to soon return to a mix of humor, fun, marriage stories, and the likes, but first there is, in fact, a recently published book that indeed does expose the true threat to America's democracy. It is an intentional threat masterminded by powerful entities who seek to move our society drastically away from what we once knew.

I said earlier I was midway through a book titled, *Canary In A Covid World*, a compilation of thirty-four credentialed contributors from a generous spread of livelihoods, medical, media, academia, authors, and even an ex-UK supreme court lord. Their shared contributions cumulate to clarify the power-grab attempted by tyrants who arbitrarily seized and somehow maintained control over entire populations during the Covid Games. Also note the readers' reviews on this book amass a near perfect, 4.9, and for good reason.

In *Canary*, the far-reaching connotations spread from obedient compliance to arbitrary propaganda, and especially versus the forceful suppression of opposing voices, comes front and center. I will spend the next pages imparting some selected quotations in hopes to convince you to read the entire book. If *Canary*, along with *What The Nurses Saw* (4.8 Rating), a book of the same order, could somehow be required reading among all mankind, we would be better off for it.

(Editing Note: I always feel obliged to promise that although I often abbreviate quotations for expediency, I won't deviate from the exactness of the points being delivered.)

Lord Sumptian—Retired Senior UK Supreme Court Judge.

A State Of Fear; Covid-19 And Lockdowns.

Government by decree is usually bad government. The concentration of power in a small number of hands and the absence of wider deliberation and scrutiny enables governments to make major decisions on the hoof, without proper forethought, planning, or research.

Within the government's own ranks, it promotes loyalty at the expense of wisdom, flattery at the expense of objective advice. The want of criticism encourages self-confidence, and self-confidence banishes moderation and restraint. Authoritarian rulers sustain themselves in power by appealing to the emotional and the irrational in collective opinion.

Margaret Anna Alice—Author.

A Primer For The Propagandized:

We are losing our last sliver of opportunity to resist authoritarianism. This is not a partisan issue. Those who wish to control us have made it such because disunited lemmings are easier to steer than independent, critical thinkers. This is a human issue. This is about crushing the middle class—the backbone of a democratic republic. This is about demolishing the foundations of a free society. Dare to question. Dare to disbelieve. Dare to defy ideology while you still can.

Dr. Jessica Rose—Researcher

Interpreting Vaccine Adverse Events Reporting System Data To Show The Harms Caused By Covid-19 Vaccinations:

A quick word on transfection. Transfection is not the same thing as exposure to foreign proteins which is the basis of conventional vaccines. We either kill/attenuate a virus or we send in proteins in a carrier package like an innocuous virus. The idea is to get the immune system to mount a response against these proteins such that an immune army is established ready to fight upon challenge with the "real" virus. But that's very different from the mechanism of action of these Covid-19 injectable products. As an aside, I really would like to know how many people of the billions who have been injected with these products knew that they were being injected with something that wasn't a traditional vaccine?

Dr. Joseph Fraiman—Emergency Medical Physician and Researcher.

The Dangers Of Self-Censorship During The Covid Pandemic:

Science is an evolving method of questioning and still the most effective tool we've devised to gain information about the world around us. When experts fail to live up to their scientific duties because they are stuck in their own self-perpetuating cycles of self-censorship, it is detrimental to the cause of science. Consider what that means on a mass scale when even the staunchest proponents of science can be made hesitant in the face of societal pressures.

Dr. Ryan Cole—Pathologist.

Observation As Misinformation:

The Covid pandemic has exposed the deep-seated flaws in our medical system, our public health institutions, and in our democracy as a whole. It has exposed the private special interests that dictate government policy, and the ties to media that reinforce that message from the government. Observing the larger patterns, we are now in a fight for our very freedoms—our freedom from the influence of state-controlled media, our freedom of bodily autonomy and self-expression, our freedom of speech, and our freedom to find truth.

That should suffice as a representation of what's here. The book is a long one, and these are but a pittance of examples, but each article in the book is carefully articulated with extensive and undeniable evidence of such outrageous facts, it will leave critical thinkers stupefied as to how we, as a people, have so dismantled our society. Yes, it is a long book, hopefully long enough to hammer home the ultimate point from Dr. Cole that our Constitutional Republic is in a fight for its life. This is no longer speculation, it is no longer suspicion, and most of all, it is no longer avoidable. Our fight for freedom this go-round won't be done with bullets or brawn. The psychological manipulation made possible by collective indoctrination has left us as sitting ducks, worsened every single time masses among us suck in for optics over rational thought. In its most literal sense: It's Showtime, and too many of us are choosing popcorn over resistance.

I'll end it here but urge you to pick this book up along with *What The Nurses Saw,* to bulk up your resolve, because there *will* be a next time.

Footnote—From *Canary* Contributor, Dr. Sam Dubé

"Fact checkers are narrative enforcers, consensus is not science, and propaganda is a hell of a drug."

May

May 02—This Bridge

For a lighter study of rudimentary behavior of the masses, let me tell you about our local Coopers Plains bridge.

Located a couple miles away, down at the bottom of Smith Hill, the Coopers Plains bridge is of utmost importance to many up here as the most direct artery to places we often need to go. Any time we hillbillies take off for Dollar General, Burger King, Dunkin' Donuts, or Walmart, we rely on the Coopers Plains bridge. More importantly, ninety percent of us rely upon the Coopers Plains bridge as we travel to and from our jobs. When civil engineers convened to plan the project which was expected to consume six to seven months, and astonishingly neglected to include discussion about a temporary bypass over the river, we can all be sure of one thing: none of those planners live up this way. When they scoffed, "Let 'em all use the Curtis Bridge, it's only a three-to-four-mile roundtrip detour," they left that roundtable well advised to remain incognito. It is a twice a day detour to working folks, plus, get this, the Curtis Bridge, the one the planners reckon is "fine," is one of the last remaining *one lane* bridges in the

United States of America. That should sufficiently set the stage for assured folly.

I vowed to keep things light, so beginning from a retiree's perspective who no longer has any regular need for either bridge, things are delightfully convoluted.

First, in rerouting already fragile motorists to the one-lane Curits bridge, the "planners" flagrantly botched their temporary traffic signal and when you couple the seditious signal with a glaring underestimation in how much traffic the detour would involve, you couldn't ask for a better playground for dissention. Importantly, even against my own disdain for agitators, I beg forgiveness, but in this case I got tired of waiting for someone else to stir the pot on Facebook so, anxious to get the ball rolling, I took it upon myself:

Not sure who needs to hear this, but whoever masterminded that temporary traffic signal at the Curtis Bridge... yeah, you loused that up. (Insert six emoji cars stacked up in a jam.)

Then I parenthesized:

(*Locals either punching the gas and running that light like the rebels we are, or else sitting there angrily stalled behind meeker motorists who won't run it, honking horns, everyone flipping everyone else off... a real study in neighborly humanity.*)

"That should do it," I grinned.

It did.

The dam burst and comments rained rapidly down, flagrant language, F-bombs recklessly littering the rankled audience participation, but most of all it was laughing emojis besieging the post wall to wall, speaking fondly to my declaration about rednecks, "We get a big kick out of us, too."

Here is the problem, and it really needs to be addressed. Locals stalled on red over here on our side of the bridge are granted an unobstructed view of traffic across the river out on Route 415 where motorists are also subjected to a temporary traffic signal. When the light out on 415 turns red, motorists over on our side of the river plainly see the traffic coming to a halt so are correct to assume our light should soon turn green. But it doesn't. Instead, while the travelers over here rev their engines anticipating green, suddenly the traffic out on 415 *resumes*!

Quotes from our side, to spare you the graphics, come laden, and decisively so with angry rural rage that would at least temporarily substantiate what Paul Walman and Tom Schaller said about us.

Naturally, the problem intensifies. The next time traffic out on 415 comes to a stop, pissed off motorists on this side without hesitation jack the gas and, danger be damned, "First time your fault, second time mine," roar right on across the bridge like old times, back when we never needed a traffic light if you don't mind.

Should anyone still need convincing, relevant testimonials reveal that even Karen has taken to running the light!

Neighbor Mike no longer even stops, casts a casual glance is all, then proceeds across, same as we've done for years. When quizzed about the uptake in traffic, though, Mike says, quote, "Yeah, fuck that. I have two eyes."

Our other neighbor, Matt, reportedly tried to sit it out but startled by a rude horn blast blowing behind him checked his rearview mirror greeted by a red-faced lady deploring Matt's obedience by displaying double-mid-fingers. Sheerly of curiosity I inquired, "It wasn't a late model white Rogue like that one up there in my driveway, was it?"

My own strategy, and this because of how well I know myself, is to never, under any circumstances, test my resilience. I refuse to offer myself to the temporary light. Instead, I hang a left three hundred yards before it, casually parade myself down the Tannery Road, turn right at the American Legion, leisurely cover the short distance to the four-corners in Campbell, take another right and without any impedance whatsoever I eventually hook up with the thruway where I gas it and get about my merry way. Regardless of how much extra time it might (or might not) add to my travels, I endure it with a chuckle. Return trips are different, of course. Knowing the light to be grossly slanted in favor of Route 415, I'll come home that way and take the bridge, but always making sure to double-check for Mike and other oncoming mavericks apt to be speeding heedlessly across, right?

May 18—The Preakness Miracle

I want to begin this improbable story by saying nobody is very accomplished at predicting the outcome of horse races. It's called "handicapping" among those in the know but no matter what you call it, professed "experts," are nothing of the sort, loudly trumpeting their comparatively few wins while more commonly shrinking obscurely into the woodwork whenever they lose, which is usually. Don't mistake me, there are indeed knowledgeable analysts and people who understand the sport inside and out. I readily respect the few widely heralded authorities of the sport and double that respect toward exceptional owners, trainers, and jockeys. Most of all I revere the awe-striking horses. But handicappers? No, and let me make my case.

First, imagine somebody yearning to fashion their livelihood by handicapping horse races. I would never blame someone for desiring such a cushy occupation, but I wouldn't blame someone wanting to call sunbathing in the Caribbean or hunting mule deer in Montanna to be their sole source of income, either. Realistically, however, people who successfully fortify their lives by means of income derived solely or primarily from a professional skill need to be substantially refined at that skill. If you would like a look at how refined horse handicappers are, I know just where to send you. Proceed to your nearest racetrack, Off Track Betting parlor, Vegas gaming room, or anywhere else horse players assemble and take a seat where you can observe the tirades, emotional blowups, and collective fury of all the pissed off patrons. It won't take long to agree there are no experts. Indeed, the best for horse players to hope for is that they are not too pitifully inept.

At the very bottom of that barrel, defying even the most basic odds that every now and then a person could pick a winning horse by blindly choosing a number, enter perhaps the sorriest horseracing handicapper on planet earth, Karen Page. I do not recall the last time my wife cashed a winning ticket on a horse race—nobody does. If it's ever happened it was a long, long, time ago, most likely at a county fair.

Hold that thought while I inch ahead.

The major aid used to string handicappers along is called a "Past Performances Sheet" (PPS) found in what is traditionally known as *The Daily Racing Form*. The PPS chronologically catalogues records of each past race for the horse indicated. Prior to all triple crown races, I download the PPS and pass copies along to our young friends Nate and Alyssa who traditionally join us for the festivities here in our living room. For kicks, I print one for Karen, too. After the PPS info is distributed I don't ask questions about how anyone else figures things, but results do show that horses picked by Nate, Alyssa, and myself, are sometimes close at the end, and all of us have cashed in on a few winners over the years. But Karen? Karen's horses traditionally break slowly from the gate and save ground, near or at the rear, wire to wire. I'm afraid she is truly that poor at it.

In choosing our horses for this year's Preakness, everything progressed according to script. I studied my available sources seeking a reasonable shot. All told, I wound up sticking with my Derby choice, Chasing Freedom, who closed mightily in the Derby but wound up a nose short. Remember, though, the Derby saddles twenty horses so who knows what all could have happened along the way to mar Chasing Freedom's late bid? All I know is at the end he was closing like a shy girl's curtains and had the race gone another furlong he would have won. Today, in a field of only nine horses, Catching Freedom drew the number three post and had a great chance—and at 7/2 odds as the second favorite, well, why not? During the time it took for me to formulate my approach I heard Karen's comparatively flash method as her tiny voice called out from the living room, "Oh, look! There's a grey horse!" Specifically, Seize The Grey, with morning line odds at 12-1, not quite the longest shot on the board, so at least a marginal chance of not coming in last.

In the leadup to the race, somewhere buried in the multitudes of data, there must have lurked a secret that seasoned handicappers and "experts" overlooked. It so happened, as the horses loped down the backstretch, the whole pack was led by, you guessed it, Seize The Grey. At this point in a race, however, nothing is ascertained, any old horse can pose as our hero. At the far turn is when to start sorting out superior horses as they muscle up their stride, surpass, and then lay dust to the heretofore leader. Here at today's Preakness, however, as Seize The Grey led the field into the far turn, I began to sense a developing miracle. Seize The Grey, finding no intrusions on either flank from supposed superior horses, went ahead, himself, and upped the ante, beginning to pull away. When not a single competitor seemed game, I muttered, albeit apprehensively, "Holy, cow, Kare. I think he has a shot!"

At the top of the homestretch, Seize The Grey had built enough of a lead to begin turning our living room into outright bedlam because everyone of us had secretly longed for the day when Karen finally wins a lousy horserace and this is as close... and I mean by a *mile*... as we had ever come.

Then this happened...

With just a single but agonizing furlong to cover, Catching Freedom burst to the outside and came barreling forth in such manner I heard my panicked voice blurt, "Oh, don't you even *think* about it you sonuvabitch," as my horse made its last gasp to try to win this race. Catching Freedom brought along with him the race favorite, Mystik Dan, along the rail where the dueling duo amped their strides for all they were worth, reeling in Seize The Grey like a dead fish, each intent on laying ruin to the whole shooting match. Oh, but look! With only yards left to cover, somehow, as if in a slow-motion crescendo of a dream, Seize The Grey dug for all the grit in his being and kicked the final grains of sand between him and the finish line back into the faces of the incoming bullies and zoomed victoriously across every television screen in America to complete our Preakness miracle—Karen had picked a winning horse.

Of all our glorious Triple Crown moments among friends in our living room over the years, where everyone cheers good-naturedly for everyone else, Karen has always been the biggest cheerleader of all. And even as we had so routinely joked about the unlikelihood of this ever happening—Karen so sympathetic to longshots—"I'll bet 'em if nobody else will,"—on this day the euphoric pandemonium that blasted against the walls upon Seize The Grey seizing the day left echoes so resounding they shall remain imbedded.

Who can say how many horses have run across our television screen, or for how many years they have been doing it? Decades for sure. But today, Seize The Grey rightfully claims his throne atop the heap of the greatest horseracing stories ever told in the Page household—captioned and forever to be celebrated as The Preakness Miracle.

May 25–Flags

Each year over the Memorial Day weekend our local Corning VFW invites volunteers to gather and head out to the area's cemeteries to replace the small American flags gracing burial sites of our veterans. Our friend, Jessica, (Alyssa's mom) encouraged Karen and me to join in, so there we all sat on this Saturday morning among the amassing crowd. Soon, what had begun as gentle conversation among Karen, me, Jessi, and her boyfriend, Chris, had now turned closer to yelling in order to be heard over the growing patriotic assemblage.

From the VFW, Karen and I followed Chris and Jessi out to our assignment, the Erwin Fairview Cemetery, where we, along with several other volunteers, split up to replace the flags.

It might have seemed a conventional process, moving from one vet's grave to the other and simply swapping last year's weathered flags for one bright and new. I had only a small number of flags to deliver, say ten or so, and Karen tagged alongside collecting the old flags as I replaced them while Jessi and Chris guided us newbies along.

I had no reason to see it coming, but the instant I came to my first gravesite the impact stopped me in my tracks. I peered down at the stone of a wartime nurse who had died in September of 1955—four months after I had been born. What jumped into my mind was my dad losing his arm at war on foreign soil in the Luzon Islands where presumably the amputation occurred in nothing better than a makeshift tent. Surely the assisting nurse, or nurses, were cut from the same cloth as this lady, tough as nails I bet, and I worked to hide my emotions. How often during her lifetime had she held strong over a wounded soldier and afterward retreated to a subtle hideaway where, if only for a minute or two, she could freely weep? My replacing her flag seemed trivial in comparison, but I still feel honored to have done it.

With each successive flag then, I paused before replacing them, trying to gain a glimpse between the dates on each stone. Indeed, I did come to a couple of more notable stops. I replaced a flag for a WWI vet, his stone sagging crookedly in the worn turf, but even after all these years his resting place stays marked with a flag to commemorate him. Next, replacing a flag for a soldier who had returned home to live a good long life, I reflected back to the VFW earlier that morning, some of the old-timers donning their U.S. Veteran caps, many limping on canes, all bearing some sort of ornate scars from lives well lived, yet with smiles on their faces they mingled about, shaking hands with strangers, joking with kids, and, naturally, saving special greetings for one another. I wondered how many were heading out to replace flags for old comrades today. Given the turnout this morning verifying how everything they fought for is still holding on in this country, I hope they found solace.

Down to my last two flags I stood at a grave where a young soldier who had fought in Viet Nam died at the age of twenty-six—an embodiment of why it shall always be unforgivable for any American to disgrace the freedom we have been handed. As hard as it is for me to hold my tongue about some of the current impudence marring our country, this was not an occasion for politics, so I replaced his flag while tuning out the rest.

By the time we had concluded our mission I still held one remaining flag. I decided to palm it. I'm sure you won't blame me. Back to my father, he never spoke much of war, but even so, there are times when I wonder what he endured. Today I felt obliged to take my leftover flag home with me. My dad doesn't have a grave—I spread his ashes years ago—so this flag will be prominently displayed in his honor right here at my home each Memorial Day, Fourth of July, and Veteran's Day. I'll place it near the road at the entrance to our property next to the boulder with our address painted on it. On each occasion when I walk out there to place it, I will stay reminded that everything I have worked for during my entire lifetime was made possible by the freedoms our veterans continue to secure for us.

Footnote—*Saving Private Ryan*

If you want to feel Memorial Day to the core, boot up the ending scene of the movie, *Saving Private Ryan*. It is an emotional four minutes, Private Jim Ryan, now in his later years, is visiting Arlington Memorial Cemetery where his family has joined him. His wife and kids remain in the background as Private Ryan approaches the grave of Captain John Miller and grippingly converses with a tone of prevailing sadness that must eternally loom over scores of soldiers who returned home to live long and fruitful lifetimes against knowing several of their comrades, buddies, and heroes, were instead buried.

You can watch the video yourself, but I cherrypicked a few comments to exemplify what most Americans are still cognizant of.

Derion Jones: "This film should be shown every year in every school, college, and university."

Mike Skeates: "My Dad landed on Omaha Beach June 6th, 1944. My Mom and I went with him and walked that beach in 1964 for the twenty-year anniversary of D-Day. I was only seven years old and didn't understand the significance of this piece of ground. As I played on the beach, I looked at my dad and he was in tears. I can't imagine his thoughts watching his 7-year-old son playing where so many perished. I've never forgotten that day."

Jim Ferris: "As I hear Jim Ryan ask his wife to tell him he has led a good life and that he is a good man, I believe we all need to reflect and answer this question for ourselves - Have we lived a life worthy of the sacrifice all veterans made for us?"

It is always good to end on a positive note, sure, but in the case of soldiers who died for our freedom, it is best to end on a realistic note. It would seem, in respect to soldiers who died on foreign soil to stand up for us, that we owe it to them to fight harder here on our home soil to stand up for ourselves. Why not make it a Memorial Day tradition, then, for each of us to ask ourselves a straightforward question. Look at our media, look at our politicians, look at our academia, look at our elementary and high schools, look at our border, look at our criminal justice system, look at our medical industry, look at our corporations, look at Hollywood, look at our city streets, and look wherever else your eyes, heart, and mind lead you, and ask yourself if what we are becoming as a nation was worth dying for.

June

June 03—Hockey Parables

    Back to some lighter stuff, one of Karen's favorite topics, hockey. Currently the Stanley Cup Playoffs are underway, and I come inspired by Florida Panthers head coach, Paul Maurice, being interviewed live by ESPN rink side analyst, Emily Kaplan, early into the second period of the opening game between Maurice's Panthers versus the New York Rangers. The first period, checkered with numbers of scuffles, ceaseless chirping, multiple penalties, and ongoing cheap shots—so the usual—set ample tone for Kaplan's quick on-the-spot interview. In response to all the disorderliness, Maurice casually grinned and observed, "Looks okay to me. Everyone knows the temperature's gonna stay hot for this series," and then sealed the deal with this beauty, "No one's been arrested yet."

    Thus, oddly encouraged, I typed into a search engine, "Favorite Hockey Stories," and was greeted off the bat with an accommodating jewel. Hockey fan or not, surely you know of the great Wayne Gretzky, unanimously considered the best to have ever played. Try telling that to Edmonton Oilers, Esa Tikkanen.

Edmonton Oiler's, Esa Tikkanen, had fished a penalty on Gretzky with a proper swan dive to the ice. Gretzky was pisssed off and throwing his ass while Tikkanen, cool as a cucumber, stood up brushing the ice off his jersey and levied this insanity: "Ah fuck you Gretzky, who do you think you are?"

The NHL is very visible, stories and lore galore, but, honestly, some of the best hockey wisecracks arise from the minors, which is no surprise to me as a one-time Elmira Jackals season ticket holder. Immediate visuals of the olden days leapt to the surface when a retired minor leaguer popped this one.

I'm not big into chirps but among the greatest nonverbal provocations is immediately after scoring a goal, swipe the goalie's water bottle from the top of the net and have yourself a celebratory drink... just be ready to fight.

This next one is available on YouTube should you wish to hear San Jose Sharks, Brenden Dillon, "mic'd up" as they say. Dillon and Nashville Predators Austin Watson collided in front of one of the teams' netminders and things turned ugly enough to call it a fight... if you say so. The footage reveals a lightweight wrestling match is all, each combatant rapidly running out of steam minus a legitimate punch ever being thrown. Nevertheless, each skated off to their respective penalty boxes to serve five-minute penalties. In what must be one of the NHL's friendliest chirps,

Dillon called over from his sin bin to Watson, camped in Nashville's penalty box, "Hey Wats. We gotta work on some cardio this summer, eh?"

Pressing onward, it grew apparent that the Toronto Maple Leafs are a primary target for hockey slurs. Who knew? The lingering bullseye on Toronto is that the last time they won a Stanley Cup was in 1967. This short story winds up shorter yet, then, when a Detroit Red Wings fan and Toronto Maple Leafs fan were swapping chirps. The Wings fan, having endured his fill of cheap belittlement of his team's current failings, stopped the bleeding by levying this showstopper: "At least our Stanley Cup team photos are in color."

Today's Maple Leafs are still bearing the dogging stigma, even if the players fail to realize it. Forward Mitch Marner, when quizzed at a press conference about what it means to be a member of the Toronto Maple Leaf Hockey Organization, unfortunately responded, "It means the world. Obviously, we're looked upon as kinda gods around here to be honest. It's something you really appreciate you know; all the love you get here from this fanbase."
Uh, oh…

First comment: "Pack your shit, Mitchy."

Second: "Gods? Yeah, that's why you got car-jacked a year ago, because you're looked at as a god."

And when the interview showed up on Instagram like a hanging curveball set in slow motion, the very first comment drew an ensuing flood of joviality from Marner's "loving" fanbase.

"I think Mitchy might be miscalculating what we fans mean by yelling, 'Jesus! What are you *doing*?"

I don't mean to brag, but I'm even on record with a locally memorable chirp levied at a goaltender you may have heard of—Jonathan Quick. The reason Quick's name rings a bell is because it's engraved on Lord Stanley's cup three times. That also explains why I don't mean to brag; talk about a chirp backfiring. What average hockey fans wouldn't know is that before Quick was ever a three-time Stanley Cup champ, he and I crossed paths back in the days when I was an Elmira Jackals fan. It's true. Before anyone knew the name of one of the greatest goalies in NHL history, a sure Hall of Famer, he tended the net of the reviled Reading Royals. Look it up. Back in those days, who could have seen it coming that Quick would leave the ECHL and wind up stifling every opponent of the NHL's Los Angeles Kings on their way to win a pair of Stanley Cups? As an exclamation point, Quick, in the twilight of his brilliant career, won another Cup as a backup goalie with the Las Vegas Knights. For those keeping score, hockey great, Jonathan Quick, has his name engraved three times upon the most coveted trophy in sports while hockey fan, Roger Page, sits in his office typing his pathetic confession of once badgering Quick with this half-assed chirp after Quick let in a softie from the blueline, "Keep playin' like that and you'll be outta here quick, Quick!" (Yuck-yuck-yuck).

In my own defense, was I right?

June 24—Trolling For Bluegills—No, Really

Noted outdoor writer, Nick Lyons, in his article *The Once And Future Sport*, dangled a provocative bait in front of us who fish, one which deserves expansion.

"Fishing a local creek in the Catskill Mountains recently, I tried to think of the one way in which trout fishing had changed most in the past fifty years, and whether I enjoyed my fishing more or less these days."

Stymied by his own question, Lyons masterfully presses forth in realizing the question as secondary, anyhow.

"I really had no answer. But if the water holds up and we don't chase crowds and we keep our eyes on why we do it in the first place, the fishing can be better than ever."

I have a friend Doug, whom I met a few years back at a boat launch and our friendship has evolved so that we are routinely in touch. Doug recently texted me, attaching pictures as proof, to justify his enthusiastic carrying on about his catch of impressively oversized Honeoye Lake bluegills. I was only mildly intrigued, maybe less, they're bluegills, but I confess to perking up when Doug revealed he was boating them by means of trolling. Trolling for bluegills? Unheard of.

I used to icefish for bluegills until I bought my boat and can now count on vast supplies of perch to stuff my freezer with, perch being the prize of the panfish species as far as most fishers are concerned. I haven't given bluegills a thought in years. But listening to Doug gushing about accidentally stumbling upon Honeoye's giant bluegills attacking his lure with resounding ferocity while foiling his original quest for pickerel, bass, or walleyes, I bought in. I already had a pocketful of the exact Rapalas Doug described, so when he invited me up to his place on Honeoye to give it a spin, why not?

The short version is you really haven't lived until you have trolled for giant bluegills. (*A relevant sidenote, NYSDEC has designated Honeoye as a site to implement a "Big Panfish Initiative." On Honeoye, the limit is just fifteen per day, with a size limit of eight inches. All indicators suggest the initiative to be on track.*) We had barely set sail when my rod lurched in such fashion that any seasoned fisher knew right off, "Whoa, this surely isn't a bluegill." Doug maintained a satisfied smile because oh yes it was.

While we trolled and repeatedly fell prey to the standard, "this can't be a bluegill," we swapped stories about the olden days. Doug lamented ocean fish the size of his arm from vacations at North Carolina's Outer Banks while I matched serve with Lake Ontario's wintertime tributaries full of massive brown trout and raging steelheads. We putted along in Doug's weathered old craft propelled by an aging "souped up" 10-horse avoiding the fleets of showy bass rigs ("the crowds" as Lyons put it), our threadbare sweatshirts, ragged jeans, rubber boots sorely lacking today's standards, a couple old farts laughing at one another while casually keeping our eyes focused on what Nick Lyons told us to; why we do it in the first place.

There is a good chance we were a bit of an annoyance to the hi-tec crowd, we certainly made no effort to avoid it. It isn't exaggerating to say we live in separate worlds from the typical new breed who steady their efforts toward constant upgrades to the latest advancements in onboard computer capacity to outfit their eighty-thousand-dollar getups all for the sake of "hawgs," and "money fish," (Lest I let my bias loose from time to time.)

The new breed would have no way of knowing how on earth it is possible for Doug and me to have spent our lifetimes landing more gigantic fish and having more fun doing it than most of today's young guns; but Nick Lyons would believe it. Even if only trolling for lowly bluegills these days, fishers like Doug and me stay passionate about proving the declaration that fishing can be better than it ever was for those who know to keep our eyes on why we do it in the first place.

July

July 04—Independence? For Whom?

Regarding our celebrated holidays in this nation, grilling burgers and popping kegs of beer are great ways to celebrate, but equally important on this day is to realize the word independence has outgrown its original scope. In 1776, the calling for independence focused clearly and intently on defined objectives, highest among those, liberty and justice for all. But declaring and winning independence is not the same as sustaining independence, which validates worries about what is becoming of it.

It depends upon who you are asking.

For instance, does a group like Black Lives Matter help or hinder the giant steps this country has made in expanding civil liberties and independence to include *all* Americans? The answer is vivid—simply remember how BLM reacted to the equitable riposte, "*All* Lives Matter."

What about today's migrant stampede crippling America's southern border? Is that invasion being carried on by decent folks merely in innocent search of independence? Another easy answer if you're asking the growing number of Americans victimized by the savagery conducted by assailants who should never be allowed to set foot in a civilized society.

So, independence for whom?

I honestly believe if you queried criminals in general, you would find them happily encouraged by their progress toward independence. Defunding police is a fundamental step favoring America's thugs; allotting an acceptable shoplifting ceiling has drawn their approval; in fact, exonerating thugs of any fret whatsoever over that laughable phrase, "punishment must fit the crime," is pure icing on the cake! Frankly, you must feel good for our nation's lawbreakers as they snowball their relentless gains toward unabated independence.

And thugs aren't the only happy campers here in today's America. Ask our nation's vociferous transgenders how their struggle for independence is coming along, as every notch of tolerance they demand is therefore *required,* even enforced. Ask our female athletes, after having steadfastly excelled in developing their own organizations over the years, how independent they feel when a six-foot-three-inch gender demented "gal" jumps in the pool and then in the shower with them. But, remember, it's tolerance and acceptance which are paramount. Female athletes, along with the rest of us, are consigned to support transgender independence by thrusting opened arms and widened doors to welcome, without complaint, biological beta males into the realm of female sports. Sicker yet, imagine the delight of our nation's fraternal order of drag queens given a green light to parade around in front school kids—what awesome sociological advantages in helping children to more fully round out their young impressionable minds.

Some theatrics there I confess, but every word true. Fortunately, most of us celebrating our independence today are still deserving of it. There are others, however, and too many, the ones seeking to "normalize" abnormalities, who are darned lucky this is not 1776, or they would find themselves drowning in Boston Harbor.

July 11—*Storyworth* Part Two

Back at it.

Question: *What is your favorite book and why?*

My favorite book, and it has remained so since the first time I read it in high school, one I have read three times since and am perhaps not done with yet is Ernest Hemmingway's, *The Old Man and the Sea*.

Each reading has occurred decades apart, and each has accordingly graduated in impact. The first reading opened my innocent eyes to the rigors of nature; the second, through maturing eyes, strengthened my ties to nature; and the third, through knowing eyes, solidified my commitment to nature.

Amid modern day's societal and insidious noise, Hemmingway's *Old Man and the Sea*, even as a work of fiction, nonetheless stands out as a bastion of genuineness by how each character pulls honest weight so readers can trust a logical sequence of events. It is a story told in the simplest manner but complete with imposing complexities to either be resolved, or else accepted. With all of that said, you understand why my recent fourth reading of Hemingway's classic, done through eyes devoted to a spiritual *connection* to nature, confirms the enormity of a lifelong journey.

You will need to read the book to see why Santiago lives on in my own life as an icon of man's connection to animals and nature, how the marlin lives on as an icon of the reciprocating connection between animals and us, how the sharks live on as icons of the connections animals have among themselves, and of course from cover to cover there is the constant sea and the endless sky, unbounded majestic icons of the astounding immensity without which there could be no connections at all. And you will need to read the book to see why, when the young boy who befriended Santiago and is left in a telling aftermath, trying to nurse the old man back to health asks, "How much did you suffer?" and Santiago hoarsely replies, "Plenty," I can promise you tears; but also that you have likely read the most authentic fiction ever written.

(*335 Words*)

Queston: *What was your most memorable Thanksgiving?*

Oddly, I *do* have an answer.

During the autumn of 2018, cancer treatments had left me as close to defeated as a man wants to admit, but here on my most memorable Thanksgiving I had begun my way back. On my plate was a splash of mashed potatoes alongside Karen's scalloped corn casserole, say a half-cup of each, and a decent slice of turkey topped with gravy. Treatments had hijacked my throat, salivary glands, and taste buds, and only recently had I begun trying to swallow real food again. But my resolve to get past this nagging feeding tube still in place should I revert to needing it, posed ample incentive.

...It took me forty minutes to finish that plate.

I still get misty-eyed whenever I relive swallowing the last bite and smiling over at Karen who caved to a trickle of tears herself. She, a pillar of granite from day one, was still strongly urging me along during my recovery. Bet your ass I was going to get that plate of food down to reassure her that she, too, could begin to get her own life back on track. A pivotal moment in our lives.

Storyworth's guidelines clearly state "you may customize questions," so I am going to expand the original question and tell you about my *favorite* Thanksgiving—a year later, 2019.

To begin with, on this Thanksgiving I was reinstated to resume my role in loading up a special holiday plate for hound Audrey. She knew something was up, evident by her bulging eyes and anxious whimpering while I went about piling up the works for her—turkey, stuffing, yams, and more. When I started dumping gravy all over the entrée she lost her shit, yapping, yowling, quivering and drooling. But if you call Audrey's plate overloaded, my platter boasted downright gluttony... and on this day I *was* that glutton! I indeed downed every bite, and it didn't take forty minutes, either, and I didn't stop at one plateful, either. But it was not due to the food as much as it was due to my second chance, my renewed perspective, and the return to a normal life that on that day ranked me highly among, if not atop, the most thankful humans on planet earth.

(379 Words)

Question: *What is your favorite quote and why?*

My favorite quote is: "*Happiness is more often found, not in how much one has, but in how little one needs.*"

Do you like it?

I hope so. The reason it is my favorite is because it's my own. Oh, sure, I am aware there might be enough rival variations to perhaps risk accidental plagiarizing, so before proceeding I should go find out...

And I did. I ran my quote on Safari's search engine expecting an array of similar takes but found only one—and might I say I landed in illustrious company. It seems my quote is comparatively on par with... are you ready... Socrates; how inspiring! Me 'n Socrates. Who would have imagined?

Socrates said it like this: "*The richest man is not he who has the most but he who needs the least.*"

Let us take a sec, just for kicks, to dissect a key element in the slight discrepancies in how Socrates and I present our common thought. Even as I unabashedly admit utilizing a huge advantage in adhering to evolved modern-day sensitivities, I do, no less, ache to envision Socrates getting his philosophical ass kicked for going gender specific.

(194 Words)

That's good for now. I am enough ahead of things, though, to let you in on my preparedness in downloading and stockpiling an assortment of these questions vying as prospective entries... "mood fresheners," call them, a friendly means to interrupt stretches of cantankerousness.

July 19—Fence Sitting?

In his book, *God, No!* Penn Jillette, of the famous comedy duo, Penn and Teller, ambushed readers with a single sentence in which he claimed, *"Reading the Bible is the short track to atheism."* I was browsing the book in a public library, intrigued to see if Jillette had perhaps pulled off a lighter angle from which to advocate his theological opinions. The answer is no. I probed a few more pages until decisively realizing Jillette's aim was simply to shout down anybody choosing to trust a pathway lined with faith. I wish I would not have lingered as long as I did. In failing to get the book back to the shelf before Jillette's hostility advanced to crassly declare agnostics to be fence-sitting, "chickenshits," I felt my neck burn as I jotted down his choice phraseology, although I doubt I would have forgotten it.

What I want people to know, because this becomes increasingly important to me as I age, is that credible atheist and agnostic philosophers find accusatory theatrics depleting. Neither atheism or agnosticism are defaulted trademarks of meanness, ignorance, nor evil. Because it is understandable that faith-based people would rather be caught dead than to be caught reading books authored by spiritually motivated atheists, I'll go ahead and reveal for the sake of anyone listening, most of those writings run cover to cover with an overall gentleness cultivated by a loving indebtedness to the here and now. Philosophical spirituality is written apart from religion and spoken minus any intention of slam dunking anybody at all, for any purpose at all. While it is true that agnosticism and atheism are fundamentally contingent on rejecting faith in an omnipotent overseer, that is not the same as condemning others who choose to see things differently. To be both contemplative and realistic, which are essentials for molding functional philosophy, it can be done in lockstep with a common principle of decency.

In that light, Penn Jillette's deliberate flunking of anyone who fails to agree with him about straight and narrow atheism is belligerent, no question. But what about the commonly sanctimonious and predictably sophomoric venom from the other side? Here is what I awoke to on my Facebook page this morning in the form of one of those placard type memes:

> *Secular Person: I want to do X.*
> *Christian: You're free to do it.*
> *Secular Person: But you think X is wrong.*
> *Christian: Yes.*
> *SP: Because you want to control me.*
> *C: No. You're free to do whatever you wish.*
> *SP: But you think X is wrong.*
> *C: Yes, but only because I want what's best for you.*
> *SP: But I want to do X.*
> *C: You're free to do it.*
> *SP: But I want you to say that X is good.*
> *C: I can't say that.*
> *SP: Why are you such a hateful, intolerant, bigot?*

When Christians take liberties to portray "secular people" as accusatory simpletons, well, Penn Jillette doesn't look quite so alone does he? The stunt of inventing both sides of a conversation as you would have it unfold, rather than how it actually *would* unfold, is a good way to get punted into the cheap seats. To begin with, when was the last time you heard a secular person beg for a Christian's approval? Do you really think the likes of Penn Jillette, or any other secular person is ever going to kneel before the cross and ask permission to do whatever X is? Christians wield exactly zero highness over any of the rest of us so, for brevity, let me rephrase today's Facebook entry:

Secular Person: Hey, just so you know, I'm going to do X. And, although I know you disapprove, I don't give a shit.

When you weigh the sum of these all-or-nothing polar angles, each authentically popular representations, you should know, contrastingly, that existential agnosticism is by comparison, a voice of reason.

From a strictly logical standpoint, despite any degree of exercised passion, both faith and atheism are contingent on belief, and belief is never a factor in things known. Additionally, belief is restricted by the slamming doors of necessary assumptions. Spiritual agnostics rationally forego belief in favor of satiating themselves with the immaculate privilege of connectedness to something tangibly known but so interminably infinite that pretending to understand it seems futile. The late Charles Krauthammer, not a man of faith (his words), but indeed a master of sensibility, amplified this when he observed to the affect that he could realize the presence of a miracle without needing to explain it.

The common assumption that agnosticism is bred from apathy, albeit it true in instances, is a woefully dumbed down version. The spirituality I know is cemented in the privilege to appreciate a connectedness to the here and now—The Known. There is nothing to believe, nothing to dispel, focus stays exclusively trained toward valuing this chance to live and meld with nature, and everything is measured by tangible fulfillment. Does anybody truly wish to contend that such a statement could be bred from apathy?

I have no clue if there is an omnipotent god, a heaven or hell—neither does Penn Jillette, and neither do you. That is why discounting agnosticism as fence-sitting is thoughtless. The exploration of the vastness that exists between inconceivable "coincidences" yet the unlikeliness of an omnipotent overseer, is not spawned from frailness or conducted weak-mindedly. *Philosophical* spiritualism, by surpassing the all-or-nothing dead ends of either/or, is synonymous with the word, "liberating," for good reason.

Ultimately, however, returning to Jillette's brazenness alongside the opposing childish passive-aggressive Facebook meme, we need to draw the line at the realization there is never good reason to dominate others via our religious beliefs. There is zero chance whatsoever for any of us to be absolute that it is we who are correct. Spiritual agnostics, by intent, avoid any such dogma, and I hope to have validated that it is *not* because we are chickenshits.

July 30—Dumb Phones?

More fun stuff, battling back against the war on English. Must I admit lying in wait for any new meme that I cannot, for the life of me, resist playing with?

When u tryna spell a big word and yo phone just as dumb as u and won't help u out

First, why does my auto-editor on MS Word no longer catch the absence of a period? Have even auto-editors thrown in the towel? I'm nitpicking but let me tell u a lil bout this phone u sayins dumb as u. Yo stupid phone is a monstrous bastion of incredibility, serving a multitude of functions. It is a voluminous library, a compass, a camera, a video recorder, it's a music archive, an unparalleled shopping mall, and it can store and organize infinite compendiums of data offsite for nearly instantaneous on-demand retrieval. Why, yo dumb-shit phone can even *find* itself if you ever lose it! There's plenty more it can do, too, including, so we're clear, correcting your spelling, even on big words, if only u could get your cobbled up version in the ballpark. Don't take my word, type, c-o-m-p-e-n-d-i-u-m and I'm betting yo phone will give you the definition, enunciation, and even say the word out loud for you. If you have the latest version it may even throw a two-minute short video ticker-tape parade in your honor complete with AI cartoon floats resembling past spelling-bee champs in honor of you finally spelling a big word correctly on your very own.

Believe me, compared to yo phone, u be the dumb one.

August

August 01—Destination Anniversary

"Destination weddings" are the latest craze. Our friends Nate and Alyssa have one planned for the week prior to Thanksgiving in Cancun, Mexico. Karen and I will miss that one. The Thanksgiving school break was opportune timing for Nate to get away from his teaching duties, but old-timers like Karen and me are never going to tempt the volumes of horror stories associated with holiday travel. We're lightweights that way. But back in May when our niece, Kennadi, and her husband to be, Joe, included us on their guest list for a destination wedding in August in Miramar Beach, Florida, we at least didn't straightaway rule it out.

At issue is Karen's and my escalating reluctance to travel at all, at any time of year. Despite each of us now retired and able to fit travel plans into our future, we have instead caved to modern-day sociological nightmares infecting the travel industry along its swath of ruin. The trouble is, I am recently on record (multiple times) losing my marbles over how easily our culture is being swayed by fear. During the Covid Games I blew a gasket and fired off a scathing Facebook post, signed off in all caps with this catchy phrase I invented myself, "STOP BELIEVING EVERYTHING YOU FEAR!"

Back to Joe's and Kenn's wedding invitation, it sat there on our coffee table for a week or longer, until early one morning, sipping my coffee, I cast a sideways glance at it. I casually picked it up and scanned, again, the fun sounding details. Ultimately, nurturing my longstanding soft spot for niece Kennadi to begin with, I let myself mutter for my own benefit, "Stop believing everything you fear, Rog." With that, I ambushed Karen as she sat across the living room scrolling her iPhone.

"I think we should go to Kenn's and Joe's wedding," I stated.

Pleasantly startled because, albeit skeptically, she had been hoping for this all along, she ditched her phone and prepared for takeoff.

"You do?" she asked, tentatively.

"Yep, I do," I stated more assertively. "The wedding is August third, our anniversary is August first, if that isn't a wakeup call what is?" I chuckled. "So Happy Anniversary. Let's go to Florida."

Karen, as it turns out, had gotten out ahead in aborting her side of our pledge to never again travel. Evidence in fact would later show how the instant Kenn's and Joe's invitation touched down here at home, birddog Kare had stealthily leapt into action. How I know that to be true is the instant I came onboard she dropped what she was doing and swiftly retrieved her assembled pile of research, maps, and information, all pertaining to the Miramar Beach area, primarily the Sandestin Golf & Beach resort as suggested by the invitation. Next, our living room erupted with the makings of a television commercial as Karen disclosed accommodations, eateries, and she even knew the local shuttle service schedules. When she spilled over to gush about the shops, pubs, restaurants, and reviews of the nearby Baytowne Village, it clearly established that from the instant our invitation arrived, the Pages would, and you can take this to the bank, be attending.

So, having already laid much of the framework, Karen said we should move ahead. How surprised are you to learn that shortly past noon we had our flights booked and paid for? We would fly down on Wednesday, July 31, celebrate our own anniversary the following day, and beginning on Friday we would turn our focus to the festivities surrounding the wedding. With our flights in order, the next thing we needed to do was nail down a place to stay—something she had already figured out, too, all she needed was a quick pitch to get me to wag my tail and come along—something she's never struggled with.

"Okay, ya happy with everything?"

"Yep."

Moments later she chattered away on the phone with a lady in Miramar Beach, specifically at the Sandestin Grand Complex Welcome Center, to cement our deposit.

When it came time to leave for our anniversary/wedding getaway, the only lingering apprehension, something we eventually decided to learn as we go, was how to go about Uber rides. Young people laugh, but a lot of us older people who are accustomed to hailing cabs aren't yet savvy.

Ours was a three-flight trip, Elmira to Detroit, Detroit to Atlanta, and Atlanta to Destin, with unrushed layovers. We touched down at Destin on time, luggage arriving intact, so we took a seat adjacent to baggage claim and put our heads together to give this Uber challenge a whirl. Karen, of course, had done all the birddogging up to this point furnishing each of us with Uber Apps on our phones, but now it came time to uncork the entire procedure. We were stumbling with it, old folks resistant to touching anything wrong on our iPhones for fear of permanently gumming things up and consequently ruining our lives, until finally, frustrated, I blurted, "Screw it," and hit "*Pickup*," then hit "*My Location*." Well, let me tell you, of all the lucky guesses, up we leapt in panicked unison because whatever I had touched lit up our apps to indicate that a driver named Dwight would be at the pickup, pronto. Off we scrambled, disoriented farm folks leaving in our frantic tracks the cornfed echo, "Where the fuck *is* the pickup," as our hillbilly eyes scanned the strange airport lobby for exit doors. Feverishly dragging our luggage in tow, dreading upsetting our very first Uber driver because of our newbie failings, our luck held out when upon blasting through the airport exit doors Karen screeched, "Right there!" pointing to a shaded covered waiting area designated by the sign, "*Transportation Pick Up*." Like seasoned experts, then, Karen and I slid fluently into place in perfect synch with the described Uber vehicle pulling in next to the curb.

"I hope you're Dwight," I laughed, nervously, extending my hand. He already knew we were Roger and Karen, so the next step was to wipe clean any erroneous conclusions about our seemingly flawless approach. I said to him, "Listen, Dwight, this our very first Uber so we haven't a clue as to what we're doing. We're sorta counting on you to fill in some blanks—we'll pay extra if that's necessary."

Dwight, a seasoned "people person," amiably entertained my clowning appreciatively.

"Well, you're doing great so far," he smiled. "I particularly like that part about paying extra."

Dwight fit one suitcase into his compact trunk but seeing the second one would be tight, he shrugged and said to Karen, "Is it okay to toss this one in the backseat with you, ma'am? That way we can put your husband up front where I can keep a better eye one 'im."

Now, to present part two of disoriented farm folks, Dwight drove a Tesla meaning our very first Uber would also be our very first ride in an electric vehicle. Jesus, everything at once!

In case you don't know, a Tesla is equipped with a full-length dashboard computer monitor enabling Dwight to proficiently retrieve real time info to map out our fastest route to the Sandestin Welcome Center.

We progressed splendidly I thought, except, and I didn't want this to come out wrong, Dwight did seem overly engrossed in showing me some of the dining around our destination, sliding his fingers across the touchscreen monitor in front of us until I dared jocularly blurt, "I know I'm new to this Uber stuff, Dwight, but how do you keep your eyes on the road?"

"Why?" he grinned. "You do understand I don't really *need* to do that, right?"

Wait! The car was driving *itself*!

Dwight patiently laughed off part three of disoriented farm folks and seized the next opportunity of a slow-moving vehicle ahead of us by smiling broadly over at me from his driver's seat, his hands waving comically aloft, his foot off the brake, and for show he topped it off with an animated, "Tah-Dah," as the Tesla dropped judiciously in line behind slower traffic.

So that's how that went.

We made it to the Sandestin Welcome Center in one piece, and from there were escorted by means of a golf cart (golf carts being a general mode of travel about the Sandestin streets) over to our annex building, The Bahia.

To explain The Bahia, it is among three annexes adjacent to the towering mothership hotel, The Grand Sandestin, and cumulatively the entire assemblage comprises what is called The Grand Complex. Grand it is. All three annexes consist of three or four floors of rentals, either in the form of Airbnb's or else more stringently monitored apartments offered by sanctioned members of The Grand Complex. The complex is a manicured sprawl of orderly courtyards divided by brick walkways, some straight as arrows, others meandering, and the landscape is a colorful blend of tropical textures, crepe myrtle hedges, palm trees, holly, and other regional vegetation unfamiliar to me. Benches, fountains, and extended stretches of rod iron fencing grace the walkways and direct foot traffic around the groomed green courtyard lawns; in the center of it all, a spacious and pristine pool area funnels tourists to mingle and converse.

Back, specifically, to The Bahia, when Karen and I opened the door to our new home for the next few days we each stood awestruck. This was nothing close to any other place we have stayed, namely hotel rooms or cruise ship cabins. This was an all-out furnished apartment, rooms radiated in sparkling ambience from lighting beaming down from everywhere, the sage green walls were relevantly decorated with a maritime and beachcomber theme, and from a functional standpoint we had full use of a furnished kitchen and our very own washer and dryer.

Now the balcony.

I am the same morning springer no matter where I awake, vacation, home, or otherwise, so it makes sense for me to have found personal hideaways in which to engage my penchant toward morning stillness at every turn. Often I must do some wandering to find the perfect retreat but, here, upon opening the large glass door at the end of our living room, I was welcomed to an arched balcony skirted so heavily with tropical greenery it created a formidable bastion that even traces of dappled sunlight struggled to peek through. Each morning during our stay, well ahead of sunrise, the assuasive rustling of an ocean breeze and the saturating warmth of tropical air, augmented the rich aroma of strong black coffee in such a way I can close my eyes whenever I wish to go back.

Of course, you can't hole up indoors on a Florida vacation. The pool opened at eight o'clock each morning and stayed open until ten o'clock each night, inviting a standard double-dip for me nearly every day. Karen joined me each morning where we lounged in the "shady pool" as she coined it, a smaller adjacent pool (probably intended for kids) from the large main one. I'm not fussy, all I care about is a place to bask in the water, motionless, "like a walrus," is how I have heard it described. At night, absent Karen and minus any worries about scorching sun, I soaked myself in the large pool where chances were better to find fellow walruses to blab with.

Four of our five days at the resort, before the pool opened in the morning, call it a sorry caveat or outright bragging, I traipsed across the complex to the Grand Sandestin for forty-five minutes on a treadmill and at least twice a day, usually three times, Karen and I strolled the brick walkways from the Bahia over to Baytowne Village. Baytowne, a four-to-five-minute walk, festively beckoned tourists with live or canned music, all sorts of cool eateries and pubs, small shops, and whatever else lends to lively vacation atmospheres.

When Karen awoke on day two, August 01, she brought her coffee out to the solarium, set her cup gently onto the table, and we sat and conversed quietly and sweetly like we have been doing now as husband and wife for forty-three years. Outwardly, we probably appeared as subdued as we usually do during "Quiet

Time," a muted but congenial backdrop to our mornings.

Nearing lunchtime, we headed over to Baytowne Village to try out a popular hangout Karen had read up on, called Slick Lips. We hadn't eaten breakfast so were early birds, entering the restaurant only minutes after they had opened. A beaming waitress greeted us, "Morning, folks, it's wide open, sit wherever ya want," and we selected a secluded table tucked back against the farthest wall. High on the wall swam a mounted longfin Albacore tuna, massive and imposing, and below it the wall was plastered with vintage sepia photos of old-time roughnecks posing with their gargantuan catches.

Our waitress, Jennifer, with no other tables to tend, was open for amiable and extended conversation so our rapport stayed steady. She snapped a couple of pictures of us and lingered for minutes at a time chatting it up. She was looking forward to the weekend and a trip home to Tennessee to celebrate her mom's seventieth birthday, a ripe hanging curveball even Karen knew to park—"You're old enough to be our kid!"

We loved the place and agreed we had struck gold with Jennifer, so we asked if she would be working the evening shift. Yes, she said she would be, simplifying, then, our decision on a venue for our anniversary dinner ousting the two previous finalists: an upscale Mexican Restaurant and the famous Emeril's. When we further asked Jen if she would do us the honor of taking care of us for our anniversary dinner she blushed and told us what a privilege it would be.

And at some point during our carrying on, Jen wound up pointing us to what became the most coveted photo of our trip when she told us about Fisherman's Cove Wharf.

"Between Hammerhead's and The Marina Restaurant," she said, "there's an out of the way path that takes you to it. You should definitely go there."

What we found seemed at first to be as understated as our own quiet celebration on our balcony that morning. But as we paused together on a bench about midway down the wharf, I snapped what I thought to be a couple of banal selfies and quite accidentally ended up with one of the nicer pictures of us ever captured. Following that impromptu photo session, we relaxed for a while, soaking up the maritime feel. After a short spell, while Kare chose to remain reposed on the bench and wait, I answered the call of the proletarian shutterbug within me urging me out toward the end of the pier where the blue waters of Choctawhatchee Bay locked down under stormy skies, accented by pelicans perched on pilings, and, of course, hovering gulls shrieking everywhere, begged me to cut loose. And I did. I, in fact, enthusiastically amassed enough shots to cause myself a bit of a culling nightmare but the lasting photo, now framed in our living room, elicits everything from wows to gentle sighs, but nobody simply looks at it.

Footnote

I feel obliged each year to keep my eyes peeled for a balancing anniversary footnote to offset all the rhapsody and poetics—this year, per usual, it wasn't hard to find.

Here came Karen and I one morning, heading back from the pool. I proceeded to the elevator on the ground floor and absentmindedly pushed the "down" button, but, oops, the only downward destination was the parking garage.

Oh, how that delighted Karen.

"Why ya pushin' the down button there, Captain?" she laughed, rolling her eyes. "The third floor is where we're trying to get to; I'm pretty sure it's up."

When the elevator doors opened, we chuckled and hopped on anyhow, having not yet seen the parking garage; might as well give it a look. Down there we giggled when the door opened, patiently waited for it to close, and then zoomed on up to floor number three.

At our proper stop, we stepped off the elevators like we had done now any number of times since first arriving, certainly enough to have grown accustomed to the righthand turn from the elevator lobby, the only way to proceed to our apartment. So, when Karen strode off the elevator, swung an inexplicable *lefthand* turn, and went breezing incoherently on down the hallway, oh what a joy it was for me to hang back there in the hallway waiting for her to halt her brisk pace upon discovering she was headed straight in the wrong direction. When at last she perceived the oddity of walking all alone, she used the palm of her hand to whap herself on the forehead while spinning around to face her error by gazing way back up the long corridor to where her favorite dope stood grinning ear to ear affably waiting for her to catch back up, if you don't mind.

So, that's how that went.

After privately spending our anniversary together, we now looked forward to the next two evenings during which we would be spending time with everyone assembled for Joe's and Kenn's wedding.

I will, of course, retain mountains of personal memories about the wedding, the Friday night meet 'n greet at the Sunset Bay Café, the Saturday night wedding aboard the Solaris yacht, and more, but I do want to share one pivotal moment with you.

We had just met Joe, but as for Kenn, we know much about her past. She has been divorced for some time and as a single mom has battled well against today's pressures, steering her young daughters, Delaney and Keller, in every right direction while implementing her exemplary model of positive energy in everything they do; all of this while she conducts her successful career. Following the brief wedding ceremony on the upper deck of the Solaris, we all convened for dinner on the lower deck. The ongoings were elaborate and festive, congenial conversation going swell, until bride Kennadi asked for a microphone to try conveying some prepared thoughts she intended to read from her iPhone. In no time flat, however, she may as well have ditched her notes, tears spilling freely, her voice quivering in the most glorious meltdown of sheer and real emotion I think I have ever witnessed. Words straight from her heart made it damned clear how badly she had ached for a man like Joe to enter her and the kid's lives. Not a dry eye in the house as they say, but the palpable message, that goodness prevails, engulfed us all and I thought to steal a glance to my left where my own wife sat so I could more deeply feel the rewards of every word the bride was saying.

And there were the parents.

My brother Ron, and his wife Cheryl, along with Tom and Michele, Joe's dad and mom, were all embodiments of restrained elation. For Tom and Michele—would this day *ever* come? Joe had waited for over forty years, he has a fantastic career, a bright personality, quite a catch, to use a conventional phrase. From the moment Karen and I first shook hands with Tom and Michele, until we hugged them goodbye on Sunday, it was easy to sense their saturating joy to see their son completed by this fabulous lady, Kennadi, who had somehow emerged into their son's life to make everything right.

Equal to Tom and Michele's elation, Ron and Cheryl, too, as Kennadi glided gracefully down the aisle, turned misty-eyed to see their daughter take the hand of this fabulous man, Joe, who had somehow emerged into her life to make everything right... again.

And ever since we have returned home from our vacation travels I think it safe to reveal my intentions to keep playing dumb (wagging my tail) while Karen keeps playing dumb each time our television stalls on commercials falling under the heading of "All Inclusive Resorts." From all indicators, I am guessing once our friends, Nate and Alyssa, return from Cancun as newlyweds, Alyssa in particular is to be quizzed at length outside of my presence...

August 26—National Dog Day

Did you know?

National Dog Day (celebrated August 26) was first established in 2004 by pet and family lifestyle advocate, Colleen Paige. The aim of promoting this day is to raise awareness about adopting these animals who are currently in rescue centers. Embrace National Dog Day as an opportunity for all dogs to live a safe, happy, and abuse-free life.
—National Today

And here I thought National Dog Day was a hoax happening whenever some prankster jacked a bunch of pictures of their doggo onto social media and beamed the caption, "Hey! It's National Dog Day!!" (Again.) But, no, there really is a recognized National Dog Day and I want in on it.

To begin with, Karen would agree with me in confessing how all our dogs have been more loved than they have been trained. This I say in deflection of recently learning that some people send dogs to "schools;" sometimes for a week or longer at a time. I doubt these are often hounds being sent to matriculate. Karen and I cater solely to hounds but I'm not making excuses. Look, I'll say it right out loud, we don't even *try* to train our hounds beyond housebreaking them and dissuading them from scouring countertops and tables to swipe scraps. What we have learned over the years is, what's the use? The most well-trained hound of all time, little beagle, Uno, winner of Best in Show at Westminster years back, unceremoniously had a rubber duck stuffed into his mouth to stop him from chewing a goddamned hole in the microphone when his owner attempted to be victoriously interviewed. But in any event, given any situation, the only accurate way to say it is, even if hounds could be trained, Karen and I wouldn't.

I can tell you, though, what our dogs do learn, and quickly, is the mastery of, "when he *really* means it!" (I intentionally use "he," because when "she" *really* means it, it does not stand for beans—our dogs have always treated Karen, and all females for that matter, as equals—I'm just being honest.) And to specify what *really* meaning it means, is to isolate Audrey's (and presumably all hounds) casual aloofness to initial commands which are always interpreted merely as suggestions or perhaps requests. I will keep this brief, but there is no sly way to explain what *"really"* meaning it means aside from example, so here it goes:

> "Audrey, stay."
> *Ah, he's just talking to hear himself talk.*
> "Audrey… I said… stay."
> *Yeah, right, I hardly see any real reason…*
> "Audrey, one more step and it's your ASS!"
> *Whoa! Yes! Okay! He really means it*!

Hubs locked—eyes bulged—ears perked. Every single time. But that's what it takes every single time. I suppose a valid case is made to ask why not just start at step three, but in practice it seems so harsh without provocation.

Back to what I just said about Audrey treating Karen and all other females as equals, listen to this one.

Recall our recent vacation to the Sandestin Resort. Before leaving home we entrusted neighbors Mike from across the road, and Christy from up the road, to arrange shifts of sorts so we wouldn't be burdening anyone with three visits a day which Audrey now needs. When she was younger, twice a day was fine, but now she needs a midday break too. We asked Mike to cover mornings and nights and Christy to handle the midday shift, or if need be, they could communicate as they saw fit to be sure Audrey gets out three times each day.

Karen and I had barely touched down in Atlanta when Christy texted:

"Hey, neighbor, do you let Audrey go into the woods when walking her? She really wanted to check out something—nose to the ground and sniffing. I could hardly hold her back."

Do you know who would never need to send such a text? Mike, that's who. The answer to Christy's inquiry is a flat no, that little snip knows very well she is *not* allowed in the woods. But would you care to venture a guess at who else Audrey occasionally tries to muscle out into the woods? Right, Karen, that's who.

I responded:

"NO. That snot tries that game with Karen, too. She KNOWS she's not allowed in the woods—she'll get her leash wrapped around every sapling and twig in sight. She has two acres of grass to poop on, that little piss pot." (And, yes, of course, I added laughing emojis—why would you wonder?)

In our own living room Audrey routinely stares Karen down in matches of will. The game is for Karen to try to unravel the mystery of what Audrey is demanding. It is always one of two things—she needs to go outside or else she is working Karen for food. Do you know who she *never* tries that show with? Right. From my vantage point across the living room, watching from the corner of my eye, their competing strategies in conducting their standoffs can be elite entertainment. If Audrey's fixed stare doesn't get Karen into motion, perhaps some accelerated whimpering and showy side-shuffles will do the trick, and if not, well I'll bet a paw right there to Karen's thigh *will*. Throughout their spars, Karen counters with squeaky chirps requesting Audrey to stand down, cease, and desist—fruitless pleas. Karen's next move? She relays her own demanding fixed stare... directly over at *me*, where I am trained to interpret, "Get this dog off my ass, will ya?"

Of course, sweetie, you just sit tight.

"Audrey, leave her alone. Move."

Yeah, pffffft. He really gives a crap about me badgering mom.

(I should mention here, before the certainty of phase three, "move" simply instructs Audrey to quit bugging people, hop up to her place on the couch, and lay down.)

"Audrey. I'm telling you right now, you'd better move."

Oh, sure, okay. Movsie shcmoovsie, he just likes hearing himself...

"Audrey, you get your ASS in gear and MOVE."

Whoa! Yes! Okay! Really meaning it! To the couch we go.

I am tempted here on National Dog Day to post some of this on Instagram to bait a firestorm from the pseudo zoologists. I would immediately draw ire from the anthropomorphic crowd, all the "how could you," drama, but in no time reinforcements from hound owners, all well-schooled at dousing pomposity, would set the hook.

For an existing example, a wise and sage dog trainer recently posted a video on Instagram demonstrating his tip on how to "properly" unclasp a dog's leash. If you do it "correctly," claimed the expert, your dog will remain obediently in place upon release. The trick, you see, is to keep clicking the clasp in mock releases so when you in fact do release the clasp, how does the dog even know? OMG! Such a wealth of essential knowledge.

Comments: "My doggo never needs a leash," bragged a one-upper. "Voice commands are all any well-trained dog should require," declared another. "My dog doesn't need any tricks. She sits while I unleash her and heels when I instruct her," boasted another. And onward marched this pompous parade of predictable prattle, each expert outdoing the last expert, etc. etc.

If you are familiar with Instagram, or any format like it, you know there is an entire segment of society who troll posts in search of those likely to enflame a warlike exchange of comments. Imagine how dog enthusiasts licked our chops over this one.

Knowing my side would be amply represented by the fun people, I didn't bother typing anything myself; no need for me to fight Instagram wars when so many others are game. Predictably, the fun people returned fire by lobbying any number of variations regarding the most agreed upon method of unclasping a hound's leash for a romp. In a nutshell, hound owners know how reliably you can rev the daylights out of a willing hound straining against its leash, panting feverishly, big google eyes nearly popping from the sockets, body squirming deliriously, preparing for takeoff. When the uncontrollable whimpering escalates to soft shrieks, it is nearly time to "properly" unclasp the leash, initiating, at last, a joyously explosive scrambling haul-ass that makes it fun for all.

In real time, the "correct" way to unclasp a hound's leash is at the crescendo of a deliberate buildup and sounds like this:

"Ready girl… are ya ready… are you sure you're readyyyyyyyyy… Okay, looney-tunes…

HERE….

WE…………….

GO!!!!"

Granted, lots of sophisticates will tell you otherwise, even shame you, and at its worst some will condescendingly belittle you. When that happens, particularly as a hound owner, you are entirely within your rights to respond by skipping straight to step three.

Okay, good. All in fun. The truth is I readily applaud, and always have, the well-trained canine breeds and what it must take to be an accomplished trainer. But among us who dedicate our hearts to hounds, we don't do it that way… and never will… We couldn't even if we wanted to. That's all I came to say; that, and Happy National Dog Day.

September

September 01—Comes A Time, Reprise

(*A footnote to National Dog Day.*)

The first time I heard the phrase, "Comes a time," was years ago during the vibrance of springtime while on a hike with our springer/lab mix, Tina. Tina and I were ascending a rugged pipeline when we heard ol' Ralph's archaic tractor coming at us from far above. Ralph was returning home from his pastured fields atop the hill, a trip presumably inspired by the bluebird morning. During our ensuing chat I mentioned that I hadn't yet seen Ralph's small herd of Charolaise heifers he annually put up to the pastures during the warm months. Ralph, with perceptible sadness, said he wouldn't be bringing the heifers up anymore. Being in his mid-eighties sort of explained it, but I dumbly went ahead anyhow and asked why.

"Ah, ya know, Roger, there comes a time, I guess... just comes a time," replied Ralph somberly. Looking back, I had no reason at the time to imagine how often Ralph's humble phrase would end up escaping my own lips down through the years.

Case in point, something I didn't want to mar National Dog Day with, is Audrey has taken her last hike. I can still leash her up for casual strolls up and down the road but can no longer chance cutting her free to run the woods with me. We each knew her "comes a time," was nearing when on a wintery outing last January, she halted midstride, wavered, and slumped awkwardly to the snow. I raced to her side where we tensely sat together for long minutes before she seemed ready to be eased upright. By the time we made it back to the truck she was fine, but both of us understood what had happened. Over the course of our summertime hikes she has shown some respiratory flareups and is winding up noticeably lame on occasion, so red flags lurk. A few mornings ago, we detoured a bit from our regular routine, browsing about here and there to scout for deer sign. At one point I lost sight of her long enough to merit a casual callout to no avail. When I retraced my steps, I found her hunched up, struggling to catch her breath, her sides heaving, and her eyes glazed. Nothing about it looked good. Over the next several minutes, even as she slowly rallied, we knew "comes a time," wasn't kidding.

Back underway we tended a cautious pace toward a favorite watering hole where she waded about replenishing, her tail swaying indolently as if all were normal; the optimistic version of having dodged a bullet. Back on the trail descending to the road and our truck, I kept my eyes peeled for an exceptional backdrop to capture photos. These would be the last pictures of her out here, so as you would expect, I spared no detail in accumulating numerous angles and shots. At home it would later take me a solid hour to narrow the shots down to the keepers, but there is one in particular that will end up defining her as the years go on. Posed as perfectly as a hound could do it, peering over a large downfallen log, the sun, as if on cue, illuminating her ebony coat and highlighting the gray etchings of character tracing her jowls and snout, she stood nobly, staring off to infinity, epitomizing the millions of reasons for never using such a disjointed phrase as, "sorry for your loss." I'll go with Ralph's phrase, "Comes A Time," every time, and consider it to be a caption well worth striving for. Audrey's long and fulfilling life may be nearing its end, but I can assure you that she, like all our other dogs, intends to leave behind a trail of all the treasures Karen and I have *gained* from her presence.

The following morning, I leashed her up and we headed for a short and casual walk up the road to neighbor Christy's driveway and back, a mile roundtrip is all. She took the geriatric clowning well, casting playful looks at me as we went. When we returned home, she bore no spite as I unleashed her and headed back out the door by myself. I have since taken a couple of hikes without her, and it's sad, sure, but never in a lonely way, and never shall be. These lifelong hikes with hounds leave such a cumulative impact that loneliness is impossible. I bet Ralph knew it. He knew these woods in the same way I do, so he knew, too, that whatever sad there is to say about "comes a time," there can only be an overall happiness settled within every footprint we have left on our way getting there. And with the gift of Ralph's phrase, I am fully at peace with my decision with Audrey; and I can tell that she is, too.

September 02—Labor Day

Do you know the history of Labor Day? Here is how I found it briefly summarized by an Artificial Intelligence Generated Overview.

The holiday originated in the late 19th century when labor unions and activists fought for better working conditions, fair wages, and reasonable hours. The first Labor Day was celebrated in New York City on September 5, 1882, when 10,000 workers marched through the streets. Oregon became the first state to recognize Labor Day in 1887, and it became a federal holiday in 1894.

Hate me, go ahead, but as with the other traditional holidays, Memorial Day and Independence Day, I have questions about a society coasting along on autopilot.

I can expound from both postures—employee and employer; having been both during my working years, I saw Labor Day realistically. The most money I ever made as an employee was five bucks an hour, but never once did I complain. I worked willingly at fifteen dollars per *day* on the back of a garbage truck at one point in my life, and showed up (almost) every day, often hungover, sometimes still inebriated, but always in place to do the job I agreed to do. I had the option to quit at any time but why? In those days I realized, deep down, that I was only marginally worth the pay, so bitching about things or blaming others seemed as ridiculous then as it has remained over the course of my lifetime. Carping about working conditions and begging for more pay is an epidemic in this country.

Here is how Labor Day might more effectively work in a free society.

First, an employee should work for whatever wage they agree to, they should improve themselves in whatever field, or fields, they wish to gain more value, and should only be terminated for insubordinate behavior. Poor work quality will be weeded out by low pay—tough beans.

Second, an employer, by default, will pay better workers better pay and furthermore realize the best workers are primed to become competition. Best to keep them on the payroll.

Thirdly, with all the "benefits" large employers are saddled with, how on earth did it become their additional responsibility to cover sick days, personal days, retirement plans, and the like? Employers should have the *option* to do those things, but to mandate any form of payment to absent employees proves counterproductive.

Looking at the slumping workforce in America, what's to celebrate?

I'll tell you what's to celebrate.

Despite lurking direness, there are still plenty of workers willing to get dirty, sweaty, and tired, while showing up day after day. There are still employees who rack up decades at the same job under the same employer. There are still workers who graduate to upper management by cultivating their skills along the way toward increasing their worth, and as far as the self-employed workers in this nation... well, you cannot fault me for celebrating them most of all.

The same kid who went to work for fifteen bucks a day on a garbage truck, who dug foundations for headstones in cemeteries, who eventually found his stride with a keen interest in landscaping and eventually dared risk the odds of running his own show is a celebration of what Labor Day should mean. Brag-brag-brag, okay I deserved that, but for those keeping score, the same kid on the back of a garbage truck progressed to learn, on his own, the ins-and-outs about office work, government strongholds, suppliers, expenditures, and most of all conducting a dependable service to customers while enjoying, for the most part, a positive rapport with employees. He went from making fifteen bucks a day to managing a *payroll* commonly exceeding fifteen hundred dollars a week. Per his own income, he mastered disciplined investing and is now debt free and comfortably retired. Coupled with Karen's equally rock solid work ethic, we are evidence that the capitalistic format of perpetuating labor to impel productivity has catapulted many Americans to achieve fulfilling and lucrative lives; I am proud to be counted among those Americans—so that is what's to celebrate.

Happy Labor Day.

September 10—Marriage Stories Appendage 8

Recently, preparing for a quick home remodeling project along with addressing a few other odds 'n ends around the house, I blundered headfirst into an awful ambush of unmitigated guilt.

Throughout her long working career, whenever we needed something, Kare typically grabbed it on her way home. A few days ago, I joined her to go shopping at our local Home Depot where she wanted to show me her preference in hallway lighting. I would, of course, defer to her in any decisions along those lines, but it is important to her that I sign on. She was happy that I was happy with her hallway light, so she put it in our cart.

"Hey, while we're right here," I said, "I'll pick up our light switches. We must be close."

"They're over on aisle four," Karen said, steering us that way. "And then we need to pick up a new eavestrough elbow connector. Clear to the other end of the store for those."

Next, in Walmart, needing a new pair of pants, I dallied for a second too long pawing through what must have been some generic brand.

"No," said Kare, "You don't want those. Those are look-alikes; the Wranglers are over this way."

"Will they have any small enough?" I joked, "Featherlight, something like that?"

So I've lost some weight, that's all, but lest I think to be the only one capable of goofing, Karen embellished a belly laugh complete with some fake knee slapping and widened her eyes for yet greater affect.

"Roger, my good gosh, you *really* need to consider doing stand-up! What a smash you would be. I'll prove it to ya. Let me go grab a few Walmart shoppers and bring them over here for a five-minute audition and see how it goes," she said, concluding a fair act herself. "Or shall we just buy you some pants and move along—up to you."

I selected my pants; it turns out they had plenty in my size and put them in our cart.

"All set?" asked Kare.

"All set," I replied.

"Okay then, skinny, follow me. We need a couple of doorstops; they're down this way..."

Alright, you get the gist. It's odd enough, isn't it, that she knows where eavestroughs are kept in Home Depot, but come on, who else on planet earth knows where *doorstops* are shelved in Walmart?

I am just now realizing she knows what's in every store and where everything is located in those stores. Meanwhile, I stumble around with a big capital, D.U.H. stamped on my ballcap, wondering how many goose-chases my poor wife must have been asked to embark upon over the years to have gained such a wealth of commercial expediency.

Plenty.

September 18—Ordinary Mornings

This morning, camped in my corner of the couch donning headphones in the darkened living room, the random shuffle of songs serenaded me in what has evolved as an ordinary routine. But even as ordinary as any morning might seem these days, I feel good for all of us old fellers who grin knowingly when I talk about waking up around the same time of morning when we used to crash. These mornings we pour strong black coffee that could revive the dead while lamenting words my friend Donnie loves to quote from Hank Williams Jr. *"Cornbread and iced tea took the place of pills and 90-proof."* But honestly, the nightlife that once energized us, well, I'm glad for it; but always mindful to add the disclaimer of how equally glad I am to have outdistanced it.

So, this morning when Jerry Jeff Walker opened season with an old favorite of mine—*Song For The Life*, a dumb smile split my face in harmony with the opening line, *"Well I don't drink as much as I ought to,"* but in the spirit of what we are talking about, during the next three minutes the song softens like this:

> *Somehow I've learned how to listen,*
> *To the sound of the sun dying down,*
> *Knowing in the morning I'll be singing,*
> *A song for this life I have found,*

You know, it keeps my feet on the ground.

...So, yeah... here's to all of us who have made our way to ordinary mornings and are at last keeping our feet on the ground. Good for us.

September 28—Marriage Stories Appendage 9

Time Is Short—Let's Keep It That Way

Enter more competing shopping styles, I'm afraid.

Neighbor Mike made mention of an overload of tomatoes in his mother's garden whereupon Karen mentioned she would happily get her canning gear around. That explains the two large boxes of tomatoes, but there is far more to the story which otherwise never would have been a story had Karen not said to me on Saturday morning, "Hey, I need to run down to Corning Building Company to pick up some more canning jars—do you want to ride along?"

I replied, "Yes. I would like that," and rose from the couch to get dressed.

Karen seemed understandably surprised at my eagerness. Usually, I elect not to ride along, and when I do ride along it is rarely without some hemming and hawing. So, what changed?

What changed is during the week I stumbled upon a social media wakeup call where a wife had asked her husband if he would like to ride along with her to their local Walmart. As expected, he sloughed the question, albeit politely, and went back to whatever he was doing. The wife didn't care, nothing personal, but as she approached her car she was shocked to see her husband bolting down the driveway shouting after her, "Wait. Wait. I guess I will go." This dramatic turn of events occurred when the husband spontaneously fell to a tremendously impactful epiphany that his wife was not simply asking him to go to Walmart, no, she was asking him if he wanted to spend *time* with her. He and his wife are an older couple, married for as long as Karen and I, and the poor man, suffering a sudden tsunami of guilt swamping him with the starkness that time on earth is short, realized the right thing to do, the *only* thing to do, was to leap from his couch and chase his wife down to be with her no matter any destination. Time is short!

Reading the post, I drew back aghast, ambushed by how often I, myself, had denied Karen over the years when she posed seemingly simple questions to which I routinely whiffed on deep-seated meanings. Especially as we get older I should, and do, want to spend whatever time I can with her.

I wouldn't say I lay in wait for my next opportunity, but when it came, I certainly did not hesitate.

Two hours later when we returned home, I said to Karen, "Okay, you go grab the mail and I'll take everything in."

Everything: Three boxes of new canning jars and a short handled round point leveraging shovel from Corning Building Company; a package of white hots, bag of tortilla chips, jar of salsa, and a coconut layer cake from Wegmans's, and from Lowry's meats, twenty-five pounds of bulk burger along with a package of hotdog buns we forgot at Wegman's.

Today is exactly one week later, Saturday morning again, and this time her question seemed to have a bit of a stammer to it—a bit cursory if you ask me.

"I'm going to Wegman's for a few things... uh, you don't have to come along if you don't want to."

But again, I leaped into action, ready with my response, "Oh, yes. Yes, I definitely do, sure I do... uh, if you want me to."

Her reciprocating hesitation, stunningly clear, a horrific truth, she really does not want me to go.

And as regrettable as it sounds, I'm quite okay with that.

I know time is short, I get it, but I don't ask her to go fishing or hunting with me, do I? And we *do* spend a lot of our time together, don't we? And you know, I never saw any follow-up from that guilt-ridden husband who chased his wife down their driveway. What are the chances he, too, mired in a fleeting sea of sentimentality, got his ass kicked for it? Well Karen and I have always been very forthright with one another so here is what I did. I came clean and told her about the inspiring post and admitted how it had spawned my own sentimentality to so swiftly agree to tag along with her last week. Kriste, by the time I was done it sounded like a confession. Next, I offered her an open invitation to honestly say if she *really* wanted me to ride along today.

"Sometimes I honestly *do* want you to ride along with me to the store or wherever," she began, cautiously. "But today, I guess I would just as soon run right down there and get back."

"Okay," I said, working to manage a neutral expression.

Gaining confidence, then, she progressed, "You know, after last week's canning jar excursion it will probably be quicker and save us some money if I just go alone today, okay?"

"Okay," I replied flatly, steadying on the middle ground, mindful not to show either gloom or relief.

Then she kissed me goodbye and erased all doubt on her way out the door—"Last week you took us on a two-hour spree that cost us over two hundred dollars. I'll see ya when I get back."

Moral: Sometimes, keeping time short is best.

October

October 01—What Gene Hill Said

This being the official opening of the 2024 deer season makes it timely for some philosophical and historical celebration of the hunter. Who better than Gene Hill, in a *Field & Stream* article titled, *Some Things Never Change*, to not only bestow high praise upon hunters, but to convincingly herald us as essential.

You and I and the game need each other; without one the other would lose a definition and meaning and purpose. As long as we are here, the wild things will be honored for what they really are: a symbol of our real evolution.

It was the hunter that evolved the rifle from the spear. It was the hunter that made art from rude etchings on stone walls. It was the hunter that formed civilization by letting others be dependent on him so that they might be free to do other things.

The songs that we hear carried on the wind are in different voices. But the meaning is clear to the one listening in the wilderness. It is about life at its most basic. It is about being strong and wise and successful. It is telling us who we are and why we are there. We learn again that without us, there would have been no need for fire... there would be no need for anything.

Humans are the current custodians of nature, a role which demands governing animals, an objective that will suffer direly should the inherent human activity of hunting ever cease. Everything Hill claims about the hunters' role in evolution is, so far, substantiated. But these days evolution is taking a tricky turn, and it should be up to all humans to solve how to contend with the anomaly that humans are the only predatory species wherein a growing majority associate cruelty, brutality, and ultimately, shame, with the biological reality that eating meat implies killing animals. Thus far we haven't seemed to approach any danger zone but there are signs.

It is regrettable these days to see humans so impetuous they cannot be trusted to differentiate between animals we should pet, animals we should farm, and animals we should hunt. We are accountable for all animals, not just some. As for animals we should hunt, the shortsightedness of claiming hunting to be a perversion carried on for the sole purpose to satisfy one's warped desire to kill animals is as preposterous as it is prevalent. I have lived my life among hunters and yes, we can be a gruff and blunt bunch, but ninety-nine percent of us care far more about wild animals than do our critics. You can accuse us of simply wanting to replenish more targets if you wish, nobody is here to prevent you from sounding stupid, but the truth is hunters carry forth more than weaponry when we head to the woods. The entire gist of Hill's article is a solid testament.

I have spent decades hunting deer, countless hours perched in hemlock trees or camped in ground blinds where I have turned days into months. Our seasons run from October through much of December during which it is a rare day that I return home with a deer in tow; a rarer day, yet, when I am not eager to go. That is why I would rather answer myself, than leave it to anyone else, to the insidious charge of being driven by perversion.

As far as my own role in hunting goes, my feelings about ending a wild animal's life are not even remotely comparable to what my opponents say about it. Ultimately, from hunting deer I have gained comfort in accepting the circumstances presented to all living things. Whether it should be an animal born to the modest joys of alfalfa fields under full moons, or a human being enraptured by the urge to go hunt those animals, life is not much longer either way. For me, when it comes time to move on to whatever awaits, I owe an immense debt of gratitude to these animals that have shared this hillside with me. Like those animals, when my time comes to leave here, I will not dare begrudge the natural way things are. My critics know little about me, even less about the wild animals I hunt; nonetheless, as reluctant as I am to forgive them for it, I still hope they might one day expand their capacity to see beyond the shots that ring out across these hillsides. In whatever way they learn it, I do hope they learn to agonize less about the truth of our existence.

As for the hunters, we already know it.

October 23—Another Year Distant

October 23, another year distant from this date in 2018 when the phenomenal people at Corning's Cancer Center pulled me through. I always reserve a part of this day to thank them, of course, along with everyone else who was in my corner during my fight and recovery—including many of you who are reading this.

I adamantly praise nearly everyone I have met who chose medical careers but shall always hold a special place for those in oncology. Their willingness to endure an inescapable emotional toll is the most gracious act, as far as I'm concerned, in the entire field of medicine. For every year I have still ahead, each next chance to commemorate this date by saying thank you, I celebrate a gift bestowed by some of the most compassionate and tough medical pros I should ever hope to know. I admire them to no ends and yearn to say so many times more.

October 26—Perspectives Of High School Coaching

Each football season Karen and I make it a point to join our friend Nate's family to go watch the Haverling Rams high school football team play. It is a great get-together for all involved, but there is always an unspoken bond between Nate and me that surpasses the scoreboard.

I've said before, the very fact that Nate is a football coach *is* the scoreboard to me. He came to me as an employee during his college days, a loose cannon if ever there was one. No need to reiterate how Nate met his match, I, too, carry behind me a solid reputation as a loose cannon, but each of us remain eternally glad we weathered our rocky start and over the years have become the best of friends.

That is why it means the world to me to see Nate down there on the sidelines taking his turn at the role of challenging younger people to better themselves. It can be a tricky quest, pissing a kid off so much they end up loving you for it. Odd, I know, but it works... usually.

Before the game we shared a quick text exchange:

Nate: Lyss says you and Karen are coming tonight. I really appreciate it.
Me: You already know how much we enjoy seeing you down there on the sidelines, N8.
Nate: It means a lot!! Dealing with some injuries tonight. Hopefully we can piece things together.
Me: You just coach. The score tonight will soon be forgotten but the impact you're making on young people's lives won't be. That's the score that matters and I couldn't be prouder of you.

I coached a year of high school football, myself, for my old alma-matter, the Magnolia High School

Sentinels. It was so many years ago I couldn't recall a single game of that season if I tried but there is one monumental memory from that season to last the ages.

Before each game, one of the higherup coaches would address the team in hopes to get them fired up and ready to play. Typical formality. Being way down on the totem pole I was never tapped for the pep talk, so was taken back when minutes prior to the final game of the season, Coach Howell, the head coach, came to me and said, "Coach Page, the players have requested that you address them tonight. I'm pretty sure you'll have plenty to say," he chuckled. Coach Howell had coached me as a player and knew he could count on a high level of intensity once I got in that room. After commanding me to take charge he punctuated with a pat on my shoulder, "Make sure they don't break anything in there," sealed off with his patented grin.

I don't recall a word I said to the team, no idea if my speech rallied them to rout the opponent, the only scoreboard I retain from more than fifty years ago is the fact that the team had requested me to deliver words of incentive. That meant the world to me—always will. So, this scoreboard I'm telling Nate about these days is the same one I carry with me from fifty years ago; the instant I entered that room the very first thing I saw was a team leader named, Selsted, suited up in his gold and white jersey adorned with the bold black number 70. I cannot recall Selsted's regular number (any better than I can recall his first name—we never used those), but I do know it wasn't 70—there was no number 70 on that year's roster. How I know is because number 70 was the number I had worn as a player... and the number Selsted asked the trainers to dig out of the closet so he could wear it in my honor for that last game of the season. Memories like that are far more reaching than anything that happens on playing fields. I am glad my friend, Nate, has the chance to pass along his ability at mentoring, and proud to always know I had something to do with it.

November

November 09—Forty Years Sober

My life prior to November 09, 1984, wasn't a total train wreck but a black tunnel was fast approaching. I have no idea what would have become of me had I not conquered my addiction to alcohol, but ever since reading the words of recovered addict and self-published author, Tiffany Jenkins, who you may recall from last year's edition, I have reiterated the way she said it because I find her words concisely on target:

"There are times now, where I will be sitting in the living room of our beautiful four-bedroom house, and I'll hear my kids giggling in the other room. In that moment, I'll think back to the times I lay in bed twisting and turning in agony from withdrawal, the times I overdosed and almost died, and I think: 'Holy shit, I almost missed this."

Every recovered addict who has dug deeply for the courage it takes to sustain the fight back to a renewed life through sobriety will, for the rest of their resurrected lives, repeatedly cross Tiffany's phrase—"Holy shit, I almost missed this." And I speak for us all when we beg of you, don't miss it… do NOT miss your one chance at life. Please defeat your demons.

Sober forty years today.

November 13—Déjà vu All Over Again

It was this exact date, November 13 in 2001, near the end of bow season, when I downed the largest buck of my hunting career. That buck is now the *second* largest for me, so I am counting on you to allow me some wiggle room here as I fully intend to go a bit overboard.

The easiest way to proceed is to copy for you the article I submitted to *Deer & Deer Hunting Magazine*. Whether they will publish it, who knows, but I feel no less overjoyed by the chance to have written it.

"Crossing" Over—Defeating Debacles

First, I want to tell you the story.

When I was sixty-six years old, a full knee replacement sealed the deal—no more tree climbing. Despite my lifelong hindrance from acrophobia, I had managed for many seasons to creep ten or eleven feet up into hemlocks from where numbers of deer failed to detect my presence; many made it, lots didn't. Throughout those years, I did, on rare occasions, win a bowhunting bout from eyelevel so my new plan to hunt exclusively from the ground at least had room for reserved optimism. Jumping ahead—that optimism has tanked, as it sifts clear that local deer are afforded immunity whenever in the proximity of me on the ground with a compound bow in hand. Scoff me if you wish, I deserve it, but spoiler alert—my prowess herein shall be redeemed.

I had an old friend, Claytie, a war vet, sharpshooter, and as a hunter Claytie brought down scores of deer over the years. One day, however, in his later years, Claytie returned from the woods, tossed his bow aside, dismayed and baffled as to how he could have missed. Days later during the same season came the same story—missed again. I should mention that at the time this was happening, Claytie was at, or about, the age I am now. Although he remained gamely willing to keep at it, he never clipped another deer's hair with an arrow. Who knows how Claytie's acute demise came about, but I can attest it was not exclusive to him.

In my own case, since descending the trees, I have been picked off by deer at a rate of six to one before getting even half drawn. The frustration is maddening, but not half as maddening as the one in six times when I have somehow achieved full draw and sent an arrow aloft... aloft being a darned good word for it.

So, there I was again, my fingernails carving at bark, trying to pry my broadhead free from a tree. The shot had soared a foot to the left and even worse high. Deciding the broadhead to be buried beyond retrieval I dejectedly unscrewed my arrow and muttered, "You know, this charade needn't continue. You have an incurable case of the Clayties, but you have many thousands of dollars in a retirement account."

The next morning, there I stood shooting the bull with everyone down at the local bow shop where it is never shameful for an old fella to be humbly acquiescing to circumstances of aging and requesting to check out a crossbow. Of course, at any age, you must uphold a certain machismo at the bow shop, some of us talk tougher than others but we all avoid phrases like "the yips," "buck fever," "too excited," all that jabber. Plus, always remember how a crossbow is one intimidating looking piece of weaponry—toxic masculinity accentuated—and when you throw in the outright chivalry of bowhunting deer from the ground, well... come on... who doesn't champion the proficient virility of such a hunter?

Minus anyone questioning this illusory veneer, I grinned and purchased my crossbow.

Let's go ahead and lay our cards straight out on the table. I've been around long enough to know what many are thinking—the crossbow is cheating, might as well use a gun (Gatling gun is how my fisher friend, Doug, from Honeoye puts it.) And that's just the start of the rumblings among other common ballyhoo which disregards the demonstrable fact that to some of us, anytime there is distance between us and prey it constitutes a verifiable challenge with any form of weaponry. Some of us are probably not much beyond the hopes of having equal chances with a rock. I'm embellishing, sure, nobody's going to hurl rocks at live animals, but as it turns out, you may be right about these crossbows.

On my third hunt, a strikingly beautiful day, bluebird skies, imperceptible breeze, I left home well ahead of noon intending to stay until dark. Midday hunters tend to become lackadaisical; it's just part of the pleasant atmosphere. Morning and evening hunters stay on their toes, those being the supposed prime times, but typical of the midday hunt I sat in my blind, daydreaming. It was twelve-forty-five, the warmth of the sunshine held me hostage, lazily pondering what to get my wife Karen for Christmas.

I would later joke to my brother that it happened so fast I didn't have ample time to screw it up. An incoming buck of epic proportions appeared from nowhere and jolted me from the poetics of sunshine and Christmas shopping. I eased two steps to the adjacent tree anchoring my blind and braced against it as previously rehearsed. From there, as quickly as you are reading this, I brought the stock to my cheek, disengaged the safety, placed the top reticle on the deer's chest, and followed him into a broad opening where I fired the bolt. In case you don't know, you do not see a bolt like you sometimes do an arrow. Given my long stretch of recent miscues, I had grown woefully conditioned to interpret a flinching buck as merely startled by something whizzing over its head. The buck leapt and fled only a short distance before pausing to decipher what had just occurred. From this angle I could clearly harness the total picture of his imposing antlers gleaming against the early afternoon sun, but more importantly my eyes bulged at a miscolored blotch directly behind his shoulder where one might hope to have placed a textbook shot. And when that beast of a deer took one last stutter-step and began to wobble, must I admit the rapid disorder of my own weakened knees?

I'm not going to leave you hanging, we'll get back to the deer, but now is an opportune time to interject the crossbow. As one who generally, and deftly, sidesteps debates about who hunts what with what, I obviously realize a hunter would have to be a complete outcast to disregard ongoing arguments pitting the crossbow against compounds or recurves. I'll ask you to remember my own original preference, even in opting to hunt exclusively from the ground, was to stay put with the compound. My decision to move to a crossbow came about specifically when I finally admitted that something had come mentally unraveled. I am now sixty-nine years old with a lingering college background in psychology, so I knew enough to take an easy way out. A stealthier way to say it is I am a man's man, old and onery; it would be unfathomable to demand a therapist to endure hourlong sessions with me. Let's just buy a crossbow.

I can expound on at least this much. A crossbow, as far as hunting goes, is indeed more in a semblance with a gun than a bow. If one looks at that as cheating, I cannot mount much rebuttal. Taking good time to aim at that incoming buck, scarcely divulging any motion whatsoever, no need to decide how long to try and hold the weight of a drawn bow, no worries about distance issues, steadying a crosshair from a scope, and as a final act of dirtiness, squeezing a trigger to ignite a rocketing projectile so swiftly that no one involved knows precisely what has happened might be cheating, might not be, but, man, what a difference! Compared to my recent folly with the compound off the ground, I accept whatever criticism I have coming but the instant I get down there to that buck and start conducting our photo session, you should know I couldn't care less about anyone's view about my method of problem solving—we all agree it worked. I'm joking, sort of, but in all seriousness surely you can empathize with my unabashed elation in at last defeating my recent debacles.

Here is a more personal take. As a keen admirer of taxidermy, I have spent a good deal of time hanging out with local taxidermists at their shops. I have seen bucks taken by everything from vehicles to long-range rifles. I have seen bucks taken from high-fenced areas or by aid of experienced and well-compensated guides, I have seen bucks taken from strictly managed private land—victims of food plots or bench rested weaponry from the comfort of "shooting shacks," and I have seen bucks taken from miles back in gnarly swamps of public land, too, perhaps by stick bows, who knows... who cares?

Sometimes I fear we mire ourselves so enthusiastically in our own way of doing things that we are prone to deride others unintentionally and even innocently for the way they choose to proceed. It's human nature, I get that, we all should, but I implore hunters to defeat intrusive noise by remembering that most of all, we are the truest form of free spirits left on planet earth. Implied, then, is we each do things our own way... period. For me, a crossbow has opened new doors through which I hope to advance for many years ahead—I am delighted by the indispensable revival my crossbow has brought forth.

    If you are new, like I am, to the crossbow I want to explain a couple of details. No matter how you plan to go about things, sighting-in a crossbow is typical to sighting-in a gun—use a bench rest. The consensus is to set the top reticle at twenty yards. That is a sound approach if hunting from trees where the chip shot is far more in play than it is when hunting from the ground. From the ground a ten-yard shot is improbable. Because of that, I dialed in at twenty-five yards and found my bolts to be dependable from fifteen to thirty-five. Even if I should get a shot inside fifteen, I have no reason to suspect enough deviation to matter much. Beyond thirty-five, though? Not for me. I suppose I've already admitted enough so I can trust we'll remain friends when you learn there is a bolt lying somewhere out in my tightly mowed lawn that nobody has yet found. That came about because of an experimental semi-offhand (braced against a tree) shot at forty yards. In the field I will always set up to brace against a tree and forty yards might be just a good guess, so I consider my backyard test to wave a red flag defining my limitations—I don't even know why I tried it. I know many hunters do practice and expect impressive results out to distances previously unheard of, but I am not one.

As luck would have it, my shot in real time was close to the ideal twenty-five yards and the result was impeccable. That allows me to answer the next question, one that nagged mightily—can I put faith in an expandable broadhead. For years I had shot four-bladed muzzys from my compound. With muzzys I could count on exceptional flights and nearly always a pass-through shot. My brief experience with expandable heads left two absolute horror stories. True each incident was my own fault, each broadhead opening in mid-flight, but I bet fixed broadheads won't do that, will they? Here on new turf with a crossbow, however, I thought it best to yield to the knowledgeable authority of a man named Dennis who handed over a package of Rage Hypodermics. I glanced warily at the broadheads, then back at Dennis whom I trusted unequivocally. Sensing my apprehension he simply smiled and said, "Come back and tell me what you think once you hit a deer with one." Here is how that went. The bolt soared so swiftly I hadn't a clue as to where it went, but the deer indicated everything certainly went well. In retrieving my bolt, I found it lodged deeply into a deadfall well beyond where the deer had stood. Trust the Rage Hypodermics.

Back to the buck—he was massive. I needed to move him a short twenty to twenty-five feet is all so I could stage keepsake photos using a fallen log with a hint of green moss as an inviting prop. I never field dress a deer before taking pictures in the woods and have dragged many of them much further than this to a chosen backdrop. I thought little of the chore when I bent and casually latched onto his heavy antlers intending to lug him over to the log. Now, I understand the consequences of age, and yes, I have been through some recent health trials depleting some of my strength, but when I tried to even budge that buck I confess to some spontaneous phraseology entirely unbecoming to the decorum of such a prestigious event. Try again. This time I reached down with both hands, gained a solid grip, and with a determined heave-ho, aggressively managed a few feet. I repeated my effort, each time getting a few feet closer until, at last, I had my photo session sufficiently staged and my GoPro ready to roll.

Oddly, it didn't hit me right away that the buck was "only" a six-point. Astounded by the overall enormity and incredible spread of the buck's antlers, I guess it just didn't register. I knew right away the spread was bizarre, but only when I got home was I able to use a tape to learn I had killed a buck with a legitimate twenty-inch spread—twenty and a quarter to be exact. I'm confident readers of this magazine know the magnitude of a twenty-inch spread on a whitetail deer better than my wife does. She sensed my euphoria, the whole neighborhood did, but as is her gentle custom she patted me on the shoulder and said, "That's nice, Rog." Yes, it sure is, honey. In my entire hunting career this is the second legitimately measured twenty-inch spread on a whitetail deer I have ever seen—guess who killed the other one... Claytie, that's who.

I need to resist my reluctance to end this—I expect to ride cloud nine for a while longer. There are other reasons, though, beyond "look at my deer," why I asked permission to submit this article. It has never been a secret how I champion the everyday hunter. There is nothing at all wrong with our moguls presenting us with fantastic stories, enviable photographs, superb information, and whatnot, but now and then I think it is important to hear from the lesser known and this magazine has been a phenomenal participant in allowing those voices to be heard. I wanted you to see a hunter who misses, flounders, stumbles, fails, but nonetheless shucks it off and tries again. As we age, we might need to modify our approach, but I hope you all continue to extend your love for the chase until it ends. As far as any arguing about the ethics of whatever legal weaponry we choose to deploy, or despite competing noise critical of one way or another, don't listen. Yours is a lifetime balanced with whatever dosage of nature you decide upon. How you take a deer is far more importantly measured from within your heart than by whatever implement is in your hand.

Footnote—Whitetail Bucks With Twenty-Inch Antler Spreads

This tag is primarily for hunters, as I doubt I will ever have such a convenient segue on which to build.

Years ago, there occurred an epidemic of local hunters constantly reporting sightings of whitetail bucks with twenty-inch spreads. It got so bad there even arose a mythical measurement of an "outside" spread—something which does not exist. Pope & Young scoring is the standard for measuring antlers and nowhere will you find mentioned an "outside spread." Antler spreads are measured solely from an inside span.

During this twenty-inch mania, I was lucky enough to be at a taxidermist's accompanied by a friend who had also heard his fill of the twenty-inch fabricators. The season being well underway, the taxidermist had a growing pile of antlers stacked on his floor. I pointed to the pile, a collection of the largest local bucks recently taken, and asked if any of those were twenty-inch spreads.

"No," he said.

"How often do you take in a whitetail with a twenty-inch spread?" asked my buddy.

"Not often," replied the taxidermist. Then, following a brief pause, he said, "Hey, wait, I can show you guys a twenty-inch spread," and he turned and left for an adjacent room of his shop. When he returned, he carried with him an awe-striking rack and announced,

"This thing has a twenty-*five*-inch spread," and allowed us to ogle a most impressive *mule deer* rack.

The truth about boasts of whitetails carrying twenty-inch spreads is how rarely, very rarely, they are true at all.

Footnote—My Friend, Tom

For the first time in my thirty-four years of bowhunting on the parcel where I got the buck, I needed help in dragging a deer out. It is typically a moderate drag, say a quarter of a mile or so to the truck, depending on where the deer has fallen. Usually, the first part of a drag is downhill until reaching a stream that courses the full length of the parcel. From the stream, everything else is uphill. Eventually you make it out to a long field where the drag gets a little easier, but the final leg of the field is the steepest so there's that. I have lugged numbers of deer out of there, including a handful of substantially larger two-year-old and even three-year-old bucks. When, however, I tell you I could not budge this animal, believe it. I have never seen such a deer with my own eyes, and it would turn out that my friend Tom, my neighbor Mike, and taxidermist Tim, all who have seen multitudes of deer, unanimously concurred.

Back at the scene there is always poor cell-phone reception down where this deer lay so I hustled excitedly from the woods and once I reached the fields I speed dialed Karen and commenced in animated blabbing. I got to my truck still carrying on with Kare while I stowed my crossbow and backpack, ready to head home to grab my GoPro and to change into lighter gear. I told Kare I'd see her in a few, but before firing my truck up I called neighbor Mike to see if he was home. I knew he would be agreeable to help me get the deer out. Mike answered my call from a tree stand, but sensing my elation offered to climb down and come to my aid. No need for that, if I couldn't find anyone else, he and I could get the deer out after dark, but there was no reason to interfere with his hunt.

    My friend Tom was my next call, and he is the one who ended up coming to the rescue. Tom is among a few other young guns who are still speaking to me despite some rockier terrain early on in our relationship. Tom is a good thirty years younger than I, and the most avid deer hunter anyone knows around here. For years he was so overtly avid I wound up worn out from watching his so-called friends encourage the annual bloodletting. He pulled into my driveway one afternoon to show off his latest kill but instead of putting on my boots I told him I'd seen enough dead deer of his for one season. I could have shut up right there and made a good enough point, but I didn't. I told him if nobody else was willing to give a hoot about him I'd do it, and spent the next few minutes opening his eyes to the idea that treating each deer season like an annual massacre appeals to a mighty low-level entourage of which I did not wish to be a part. When I concluded with a suggestion that he strongly consider getting his act rearranged, he shocked me with an agreement to try harder. Given his receptive reaction despite the likelihood of my having gone (way) overboard, I relented, slipped my boots on, and went out to see his deer. Face it, my intervention that day took a lot of balls, but not half the balls it took for Tom to resist punching me in the face... I suppose.

There have been a couple of other times, too, where I've taken minor risks in uninvitedly mediating this or that with Tom, but each time I've done it he has responded rationally rather than defensively. It's impressive as all get out if you want the truth. But for years I was dismayed that he hadn't a single friend his own age who knew enough to step in at times. Both of his parents have passed, I have lost track of his brother who might otherwise be helpful, so every time I've felt compelled to contribute my two-cents I am saddened to be, apparently, the only person on earth in his corner—methods be damned.

But those days are behind us now. Our friendship has evolved, and thankfully his new girlfriend, Kara, and her daughter, Faith, have taken the ball in giving Tom a more fulfilling life. Their relationship has advanced to moving in together, hunting together, and just to know Tom recently said to me during the first week of an open season, quote: "I can't hunt Friday. Faith has a cheerleading competition in Owego," is a solid indication of his progress. He is totally immersing himself in their lives proving to be, in fact, one of the more unselfish people in our world... who knew?

Over the past few years, he has helped me with several deer. We hunt the same woods during gun seasons where Tom is always game to fire up his four-wheeler to come and get my kill. But the buck we're talking about in this instance was a bow kill on property where four-wheelers are forbidden and, also, Tom was fairly warned over the phone to suck down a few energy drinks—and are you sure you really want to do this?

To show how far we've come, Tom replied that he could not wait to get there—"Anytime, anywhere," he said, "You just gimme a call."

During the drag, we stopped intermittently for breathers wherein I took opportunities to reiterate my appreciation for not only his help with this buck, but, too, in the many ways he has continued to grow and progress. A customer of mine once complimented me by prefacing, "It's always nice to hear the good things, too," and recalling how uplifting the phrase was to my own ears I thought to incorporate it myself any time I have a chance. It's no secret I nurture a soft spot toward young rebels who eventually master stability on their journeys toward becoming dependable men and women, particularly those who endured my "input" along their way. So, I admit to some tightness in my throat when Tom, in his own roughneck lingo, said back to me, "Yeah, well I owe a lot of it to you. You was the one who told me Kara was making things pretty obvious when I was ghosting her, and you was the one who told me how to take pictures of deer, and you was always tellin' me straight out how things was. That means a lot and I'll help you with deer any time anywhere, you just give me a fuckin' call."

Of all the oratory perfection I have commended from polished speakers, and of all the eloquent ways I have strived to project my own thoughts, I bet you can guess I grinned and let Tommy's exposé slide wall-to-wall.

I chuckled and humbly replied, "I'm not sure you could possibly realize how much it means to me to hear all of that, Tom," as I latched back onto my side of antlers to resume our climb to my truck.

"Well, it's all fuckin' true," he accentuated, assertively, latching onto his side of the antlers and contributing mightily to this story which I intend to read back to myself over, over, and over again down through whatever years I have left.

November 28—Thanksgiving

If you could hold on to just one memory of your life forever, what would that be?

And Part Two:

What qualities do you most value in your better half?

More *Storyworth* questions, these purposely kept locked and loaded specifically for this day. The first of the two questions should ordinarily be quite impactful, challenging one to a single memory to hold onto forever, but my answer required zero thought. I muttered on the spot, "Oh, that's easy." It is a memory concretely secured as the auspicious turning point that made the rest of my life so much more than worthwhile.

The most lasting memory of my life, the one I will hold on to until the end, came shot from the hip of a nineteen-year-old girl who became my wife. I have told the story enough to hustle along the abbreviated version, here, but if this were my only chance as an old man answering a yearlong selection of questions, the unhurried versions of these two would leave behind assurance that the whole family, from current ancestry to trailing lineage, would surely get their story's worth.

Karen and I each worked in the hotel industry in Anaheim, California where one night in a roundabout whirlwind we were thrown together in conclusive evidence of fate. Tour guides stationed in each local hotel had offered complimentary tickets to a handful of employees from those hotels to be their guests on a new tour they were offering, the end game obviously being we would trumpet the tour to future hotel guests. The tour, a nighttime champagne cruise sailing out of Newport Harbor, canvased the homes of famous people and places, the highlight being John Wayne's impressive home overlooking Balboa Island. I worked as a bellman at a Holiday Inn, Karen tended front desk duties at the nearby Hyatt House. We each recall exchanging quick hellos on the upper deck that evening, and each recall, too, how dummy me was currently infatuated by a more flamboyant chick, or, "little whore," is how Karen remembers her—I've never rebutted. Two hours later when we all boarded the bus to head home, the first empty seat I came to was next to Karen. Meanwhile, the little... the other girl... sat a few rows ahead, so Karen, either sympathetically or sarcastically, (doesn't really matter now, does it?) looked up at me and said, quote: "Do you want me to switch seats with her?"

In response, despite the influence of alcohol, despite the despondency of a recent divorce, despite knowing I was leaving California in ten short days, and despite everything else that might have otherwise caused me to botch my part, I instead pulled off the greatest save of my entire life when I smiled back and replied, "No. These seats are fine... In fact, they're *very* fine." (Insert uproarious applause and wipe away a tear.)

That is the general memory, but I am sure *Storyworth* would oblige in letting me fine tune the lasting memory, the one I am blessed to constantly carry.

Her eyes.

Specifically, the instantaneous and resolute connection between the two of us when she cast her innocent eyes, glimmering even in the dim lighted bus, directly up at me, made very clear that the *last* thing she wanted was to switch seats on that bus. I'll try to convey it this way—her question, "Do you want me to switch seats with her?" came intercepted by the fate just spoken of and was then adeptly relayed through Karen's soft chestnut-colored Norwegian eyes that *dared* me to answer wrongly, while at the same time pleading that I wouldn't.

The second half: *What qualities do you most value in your better half?* I admit to parlaying myself, the two questions so seamlessly intertwined.

The answer to part two is all-encompassing. The qualities I most value are how neither of us look at the other incrementally. I value the entire essence of my wife, as she does me, we are the whole of two halves, yes, but with no dividing line—there's a difference. But a few things do stand out. I value how she has never said, "Well if you're going to do that, then I'm going to do this." I value how she has never said, "I don't need a man for that, I can do it myself." I value how she sometimes worries about me, even when she doesn't need to. I value how she lets me be a man and is proud of the man I am, and I especially value how proud she is of the way I see her as a woman and a wife.

I could carry on for hours, but in a nutshell, what I value most of all about my better half is all the good that has happened in our lives because back on that bus she somehow saw in me what, without her, I may have never ended up seeing in myself—and forever knowing she had no intention, whatsoever, of switching seats.

December

December 08—Marriage Stories Appendage 10

Preparing For Kitchen Remodeling

Excitement mounting, tomorrow begins our long-anticipated kitchen remodeling project. Back in midsummer I hinted to Karen how I thought our cabinetry was looking shoddy and asked for her thoughts on doing some refinishing or maybe even going the distance and having new cabinetry installed. You can probably guess her input was neither casual nor did it take a fortnight. Before the hour was up I, per instruction, had contacted our friend and contractor Jason to invite him over to our house to sketch a plan for new cabinetry. We scheduled our appointment, Jason showed up, and our ensuing discussion about kitchen cabinetry rapidly escalated. Karen is why, pretty sure she'd planned it, but I admit to offering zero resistance. Face it, who isn't interested to hear about what's new in kitchen countertops as well as cabinetry? And as long as we're to swap out our old countertops for the latest in quartz, that implies our antiquated old stovetop and island are next, right? Not only that, but naturally, too, a new sink adorned with a contemporary brushed satin nickel faucet all backed with a decorative new backsplash should be added to the inventory. Well, then, what about the adjacent pantry—isn't that a part of the kitchen? Why hell yes it is! A dark pantry at that, and so 1970's (my god, we still had paneling in there) so what's the holdup on incorporating that mess into the project and get it updated to the current century? Back in the main kitchen area, the project now rampantly unleashed, who in the world these days wants a giant old-fashioned kitchen table and chairs hogging up all that space over by the far wall? Best to ditch those in favor of a swank coffee buffet and go with the new trend of staging modern barstools at the kitchen island overhang. Fully onboard now, it was me who pointed up to the track lighting and wondered aloud if recessed lighting wouldn't be preferable. Oh, you bet your life it would... and then I told Jason we had track lighting in several other rooms and he said why don't we just replace every goddamned one of 'em, which prompted me to inquire about adjustable angled ones for my office to give the taxidermy the exquisite accentuating it deserves. Jason said those were a bit more expensive, but he could get them. Expensive? What on earth could that (apparently) have to do with any of this?

Here is where to insert a tardy but brief prologue to all of this. Karen's and my living arrangements originated back in an efficiency apartment. From there we advanced to a decade of trailer life, and when we moved to our home here on Beeman Hollow, thirty-four years ago, the term "fixer-upper" never had it so good. Most importantly, every step of our way has been hand in hand, which is to say we are quick to compromise on every aspect of every home improvement we have made over the years. We have each said we would live in a tent together if need be, and we seemed damned close to it, too, back in the days when during wintertime we used to staple heavy plastic sheeting over our windows and sometimes call upon our kitchen oven for supplementary heat. So, today, and I don't mean for this to sound naïve, nor arrogant, but when the issue of cost came up between us, we each, again, compromised by shrugging, smiling, and agreeing, "Let's just do it and find out."

Back to business, the next step was for Karen and me to head downtown to Corning Building Company and introduce ourselves to Jason's trusted liaison and home interior specialist, Erin. Erin would guide us from the groundwork of implementing our basic ideas into a coordinated plan. As far as minor specifics, we agreed to get away from the graininess of the current oak veneer in our kitchen and move to a smoother and lighter contrast of maple. The countertops and backsplash, too, took little deliberation, I lobbied for a split double sink, she nixed a soap dispenser, the black stovetop is fine, and at this point Erin good naturedly chuckled and said, "You guys are *easy*!" There were a few loose ends is all, paneling style, door handles, the sink faucet, routine stuff, before Erin at last closed her folder and said, "Okay, the next step is for me to come out to your house, take some measurements, and draw up a design."

And since then, everything has moved along according to schedule. Orchestrating a project of this magnitude takes a lot of time and planning, but at last the predetermined start date of December 9th is upon us.

Now, if you were expecting, by "marriage story," something more in line with the typical sit-com, I haven't forgotten. I realize this comparatively sentimental entry has fallen shy of that but let me work to salvage your trust.

Like most kitchens and pantries, our old setup included areas of varied usage. Some areas were frequently used, some were sometimes used, and some were essentially forgotten. Sound familiar? Why, of course it does.

Before commencing with our remodeling, each inch of our old setup must be stripped bare, requiring Karen and me to join forces here on the weekend prior to takeoff in clearing everything out.

To me, it seemed an opportunity to rid ourselves of a gross accumulation of rarely or never used spillovers from years past; a fresh chance to reclaim a state of organization. But while I prepared to open season on cleaning house, Karen ambushed me with a stroll down memory lane earmarked by a nostalgic mission of rediscovery and recovery.

(And here I said how well we get along.)

"Oh my gosh, look at this cute deviled-egg tray (1993), I'd forgotten all about it!" she started. "Oh-oh, look! Our bread making machine (1996). Oh wow! Did you know we have a deep-fat fryer (1997)? Roger, look at all these beautiful flower vases (1989-2004)! Oh-oh-oh, how did I misplace this handy triple-cup snack server (2003)?" Etcetera-etcetera and so on and so forth... you get the gist.

I succumbed; it would, after all, take a hardened heart, indeed, to discourage her fun. She, on the other hand, may have sensed herself being a little gushy so she did let me trash enough to keep the peace. And I don't know if it was overcompensation, but out of the blue and minus any provocation at all, she went full redneck in declaring, "I'm trashing half of this crap outta the junk drawer, but in our new kitchen the junk drawer's going right back exactly where it was before."

Right. Understood and uncontested, but isn't it the funniest thing, knowing the term, "junk drawer," requires no expanded explanation. Old kitchen, new kitchen, cluttered or cleaned, we all maintain our own version of the universal junk drawer... aka, "shit drawer" in lesser regions.

December 18—Seasons End

The deer season closed yesterday at civil twilight. It was down to muzzleloaders anyhow, and I haven't heard a shot in days. This morning, I leashed Audrey up for our one-mile geriatric stroll up the road and back.

She's deliberate in her ways, slowing here and there to sniff every square inch of anything that catches her curiosity, and I adhere to whatever pace she desires. Her breathing is a bit coarse, her gait is still spry enough, though, notwithstanding a slight drag on her left hind leg, and her tail sways in defiance of the things cluttering my mind about her health. She has a sore under her chin that bleeds now and then, so I take whatever blankets that need washing down to the basement to the washer and dryer and while down there I can let a few tears free that always come at some point in the lives of dogs and us who love them. I'm guessing before long the tears will stream unabated for a day or two, but in the long run nothing about any of that deters the ultimate bliss we have known from sharing such love for as long as it lasts. There is never a sense of loss; the notion, in fact, seems silly. When Audrey departs it will be the beginning of multitudes of happy memories which would otherwise never have been known—her last breath, whenever it comes, will not in the least obscure everything gained through our long companionship.

That is what I was thinking about as she and I walked this morning. After our walk together I would head out alone for the annual "day after deer season" ceremonious hike, where typically the hound, after having been cooped-up for months, at last bounds free back out into the wild. But Audrey, for her own good and mine, is denied the woods from here on, something that saddens me more than it does her. Honestly, she couldn't care less; these morning walks of ours sufficiently ignite her euphoria. This morning when we returned home she performed her ritual of scarfing down her chicken breast/kibble breakfast, slurped her fill of water, and slumped to dreamland on the couch, giving zero thought to me descending the steps to our basement where I got dressed for my hike.

Without her, I took off and headed for a ground blind newly set up this season. I need to do more intricate scouting for just the right spot. That's how it always goes. You narrow a likely area down to a chosen spot, the right feel, good vantage point, but after a hunt or two you nearly always seem prone toward an incremental move. Sometimes the second move evolves onward to a third or even a fourth move. This, of course, applies primarily to us who do not own land and cannot easily influence the deer by governing food plots or cleared pathways, and whatnot. The way I hunt deer, and would choose to anyhow, is by studying them and deciphering what they are telling me. Even as I write articles about hunters downing deer caught in wide open fields feeding in front of shooting houses, I no less insist on doing things my own way when it's my turn. I like *hunting* deer and personally will never lure them. As an ambush style hunter, making moves to get closer to deer is better for me than camping in a comfy enclosure and bench-resting a rifle to shoot across open fields.

I've drifted way off course from what I came to say. My reason for today's hike was to, one, immerse myself in the winter woods, a new inch of snow having fallen overnight, and two, to scope out how to set up where I need to be next season with intentions to shoot a deer at twenty-five yards with my crossbow. My current setup is good for a rifle, but I need to move further down the hill for the crossbow.

The woods on the day after deer season have always been festive for me, the dog's unbridled and infectious glee following months of sequester sees to that. Without a dog along, however, the winter woods are a bastion of hushed silence, saturating in fact, but not in a bad way, not at all. This year I found what I always do, an idyllic backdrop for a private celebration, but I also knew, because I have come out here specifically for it from time to time, that these woods are the kindest place on earth for a hurting heart— where a man can agree that although seasons end, that is no comparison to the seasons that were; and here, again, I am speaking of Audrey.

I wonder how many reading this have ever gone far enough away, and stayed there long enough alone, to distinguish beyond the shallow versions of convincing and believing—nothing read, taught, or preached—the plain sight that everything in life, even against the certainty of death, is appropriately measured in gain; never loss. If you haven't done that, and are thinking about it, now, a good place to start would be amid the hush of the winter woods.

When I returned home to Audrey, I chuckled at her snoring in slumber, her legs and paws flinching in pleasurable dreams, her tail thumping now and then against the couch where she laid, and I wonder if somehow she might have joined me out there, today, if somehow maybe she knew. Probably not, but what I can positively say about Audrey's frequent dreams these days is they are all good ones—happy and pleasant—after all, throughout her twelve-and-a-half years, that is all she has known. Her seasons shall eternally remain celebrated as exquisite.

December 19—Marriage Stories Appendage 11

Competing Perspectives of Falling

What a sudden, unexpected, and dreadful feeling! On autopilot, I ascended two steps up onto a small ladder to perform a mundane task, simply up there to rehang a mounted trout back up onto my office wall. The new lighting is now installed, and it inspired me to do the annual cleaning a couple months ahead of schedule and this fish was the final one to be spiffed back up. Despite the short duration of the task at hand, a few seconds is all, boy did I swiftly wake up on the way back down when I discovered my aging mind had temporarily recorded only one step of the ladder, not two. I abruptly realized the error when my left foot, coordinated with said aging mind, instead of landing firmly upon the laminate flooring, kept right on going. Meanwhile Karen, and this will shortly be unfortunate in so many facets, had already begun swiveling from her spot on the living room couch from where she was afforded an unobstructed view of where I was currently airborne. I had involuntarily alerted her of my misstep by means of primal verbalizing my shock of omitting that lower step. Despite being afforded a plain view of her airborne husband, she was in fact too late to witness the fall itself. She is older now, too, so her dwindling reflexes aren't much to brag about. But she saw enough, and in the aftermath claims to have seen me, quote: "literally bounce" off the floor. She might be right, too. I know from my own view, before I could even assess preliminary damages, Karen's bizarre expression resoundingly flashed before me akin to what I suspect will be the last thing on earth I shall one day see.

    It is rare for me to have a witness when I fall, so lots of people would be surprised by how practiced I am at it. Karen's shock was understandable, she has no inkling of how tightlipped I can be, but in this case, my fall being so in-your-face she saw me bounce, how could I convince her this was lots easier than what I am accustomed to... namely the luxury of a flat surface to light upon. Generally, my private falls are spontaneous somersaults out on the jagged terrain in the middle of nowhere. Those are showier and more spectacular, agreed, but as I am saying, this one wasn't exactly chopped liver, evident by my incoming wife, rushing fervently in panic, her fingers probably already hammering out 911, and her voice in such a pitch (I can joke about it now) that I was surely glad to be minus my hearing aids upon impact...

Alright, I'll stop.

But now that it's over there are some lasting relevancies on how the two of us part ways on how to view a fall (so long as they are *my* falls.) It is two days later, now, and Karen is still inspecting me for bruises although none are forthcoming. She remains in dire search for a hematoma, secretly hoping for me to learn my lesson before it's too late.

Honestly, she was simultaneously equally relieved as she was pissed when she hovered over me worried sick until I, realizing I was okay, let her lend a hand to my elbow to help me upright where I grinned and declared, "Can you believe I can still bite the dust like that and bounce right up. I must be in terrific shape for my age, eh?"

No way would she subscribe to anything humorous about this, to the contrary she shook her head and scolded, "You think it's funny how you keep trying to convince me you're Superman, but it's *not*... and *you're* not!"

"No, no, it's not like that at all," I replied, raising my hands defensively, "I don't fall on *purpose* for krisesakes, I'm not a stuntman," and I gave her a few seconds to be satisfied with that.

"Are you sure you're okay?"

"Lookit, me," I replied, and feeling confident she might be open to laugh it off with me I added, "I think even Superman would be impressed by a feller my age hopping up unscathed from a face-plant like that, don't you?"

Apparently not...

So, that's how that went.

December 25—Merry Christmas

I hope you will receive my Christmas tidings with good cheer. And Merry Christmas to me, too—I love these things.

Which shall we unwrap first...

Let's do a couple at once; these two were posted within minutes of each other by separate friends on Facebook and offer sound testament to the vast parameters of which I can reach out to maintain "friends."

First:
Nature is my religion.
The earth is my temple.

Followed by:
I ain't feel shit the earth know who to fck with and who not to

I couldn't make up the curious timing of this one-two punch of competing memes even if they occurred on Earth Day, which they did not.

With my friend who posted first, I join her at least in part, finding in nature a spiritual connectedness beyond the boundaries of belief or faith, where there is no exercise of convincing or outward display of supposed preeminence, no debates about who is wrong or right, no judges, and most of all no applicable acuity wasted toward explanation. The core of spirituality is to stay free from noise anywhere beyond your own heart, mind, and eventually, soul. Humans are free to believe whatever comforts them about the unknown, but some of us benefit from an unabated liberating freedom of simply trusting it.

The second post is lighter fare. The friend who posted is not prone, surprise-surprise, to engage in intricate conversations; her entry here is but one of many similar. She is prone, however, toward prolific conversations, nearly always off-color and silly, but during one memorable candid interlude between us I was adorned with a lofty "compliment" from her that went (verbatim) like this:

"I wish I could talk sweet like you, but I don't know all them fancy fuckin' words."

I will point out, too, that throughout her genuine compliment she spelled each word, including the misused ones, correctly and inserted punctuation. Now, as far as her nonsensical meme goes, you can speak up if you dare but let me assure you about the earth knowing who to fck with and who not to, take my word, every one of us on earth are wisely advised to *never* fck with her. As a relevant sidenote, I hope to be correct in assuming she will never read this. (She won't.)

Let's unwrap one more from her to prove how dependable she is toward the in-your-face type of meme... that and because she's just a fun person in general.

Not everyone is going to think you're gorgeous, amazing, and magical.
They're wrong though.
Dickheads.

I don't have anything analytical to add here.

What's next? Ah, geez, this one on Christmas?

"We can ignore reality, but we cannot ignore the consequences of ignoring reality"—Ayn Rand.

We cover this repetitively, but I haven't seen it worded so eloquently.

Any time a biological male drives a volleyball against the face of a female on the other side of the net and she is then carried off the court—that's a consequence of ignoring reality. When a foreign lowlife saunters through our opened borders and in enjoying his new freedom stalks, attacks, rapes, and then kills a college student out for a morning jog across her campus on her way to a bright future in *her* country—that is a consequence of ignoring reality. When a business owner is ambushed by a mob of deviants who smash the store to bits and take whatever they want without suffering any repercussions whatsoever—that is a consequence of ignoring reality. When half a society parades about in masks believing it to be, in any way at all, an effective measure to thwart a virus—that is a consequence of ignoring reality. When the true criminals in our government blatantly assault political opponents with phony charges and get away with it, when our own FBI is a coverup agency, when our IRS selectively seek their marks from a political perspective, when our DOJ is staffed wall-to-wall with conniving white-collar goons, when governors of states assume arbitrary rule to mandate demands they, themselves, have no intention of adhering to, when your entire nation is folding to an autocratic takeover by a collection of bottom-dwelling tyrants—that is a consequence of ignoring reality.

I'll stop, but you see why I applaud Ayn Rand for her eloquence—I can't do it that way.

… We need another fun one.

Yeah, I've tried shutting up.
It's not for me.

Right away I thought of my friend, Diane, a noted introvert with whom I hope to have slowly made amiable inroads with over the past couple years. Di is the one who provided the meme to end last year's book—remember this pearl:

Humans*: Dear God, please let 2024 be a good year.*
God*: …Wait, you guys are still alive??*

She is a cerebral sort, for sure, and I honestly think she's okay with my lighthearted observations about her introverted nature, but to be safe I am also quick at self-deprecating my own quirks caused from being, "such a damned extrovert all the time." That last quote is Karen's not Diane's, but I'm not blind—it is a general quote agreed upon and levied from most anyone who knows me, but one I continuously laugh off and have ducked for years while having (so far) kept shy of ever calling anyone dickheads over it. I also know everyone makes fun of my blinking and facial contortions, too, but I would find them to be a bit weird if they didn't.

Back to Diane, I could not wait to send this meme to her, a tidily giftwrapped hanging curve ball for her to park if she so desired. I can't recall what she did with it so she must have taken it easy on me, but when I shared it on my public timeline the response was decisively in testament that my blinking isn't the only thing friend's notice. Despite all the witty comments I accrued, I still think Karen's phrase, "Running for mayor," to personify my enthusiasm toward conversing with others, whether they like it or not, is hard to top.

What else do we have? How about this quick stocking-stuffer:

Therapist: 'And how do we respond when someone calls us a trainwreck?'
    Me: *Pumps fist* 'Choo-choo!'
    Therapist: 'No.'

And we always save the best gift for last. This one comes adorned with a giant bow, donated from my fellow redneck buddy, Donnie; it's a full minute long video of an Australian "family dispute," taking place out on some lightly traveled roadside and against the backdrop of Waylon Jennings' old classic Dukes Of Hazzard theme. It's a wonder someone didn't get hurt, the boys brandishing tire tools and chain cutters, the girls deploying a bunch of near-miss face slapping bluffs and equally anemic "karate" kicks missing by a mile. The middle fingers and outrageous screaming and yelling seem impactful, I guess, and at its crescendo one of the hillbilly chicks jumps into the driver's side of the family's temporarily vacated parked truck as if to heist it but before she can master ignition her brother, husband, dad, or second cousin, whoever he is, crawls in behind her and shoves her ass on across the seat where another of the boys has dashed to the passenger side door in anticipation, grips her arm, and hauls her right on out the other side. Pretty smooth. She's pissed and gives him the finger. Onward, then, it plummets, a redneck scene straight off the farm exhorting Donnie, a creative guy to begin with, to caption it like this: *"When the fam goes 'Full Trailer Park."* The video was fine enough on its own to watch a couple of times, but I suspected the comments would add dramatically and of course they did. Most were as witty as expected, "At least nobody had to worry about getting their teeth knocked out." Or, "What would have started this—a DNA test revealing which brother was the father to which sister?" And, "It was the hillbilly Kung-Fu shit for me." All good, but ultimately, I landed upon one which we can call the showstopper, the quintessential gift that promises to keep on giving:

I forget how helpless the average human is.

You can almost hear the accompanying somber sigh.

December 31—Resolutions Ongoing

New Year's resolutions are innocent enough, but meaningful resolutions are not achieved in the moment; they evolve over a course of time to add to the mapwork of a person's emergence until life ends. How your life unfolds is generally a strong indicator of your sincerity about resolutions. There is a song called *Reno and Me*, written by Kevin Welch and John Hadley and recorded by Waylon Jennings in which the following lines challenge one's scope of perspective.

"What's the point of a race where you stay in one place, believing there's somewhere to go?"

And:

"Climbing a ladder that leads to a hole in the ground."

At first glance, from a strictly lyrical standpoint, the lines are creative and do entice thought. In practice, however, if so little matters between cradles and graves, our life merely a purposeless race enroute to a hole in the ground, why on earth bother with resolutions?

Maybe the truth is the race and ladder are each evidence *of* our destination. It is not a senseless opinion (I surely hope not) that our destination is to be born as a new link to an ongoing chain, and we race and climb the ladder as matters of interaction, seeking to better ourselves as matters of appreciative integrity—we receive our lives as priceless opportunities, the odds of each individual invitation on par to winning the lottery. English writer and poet, Mervyn Peake, said it well:

"To live at all is miracle enough. The potential people who could have been here in my place but who will in fact never see the light of day outnumber the sand grains of Arabia."

If those words do not clarify absolute viability to the point of a race and logical incentive to climb the ladder, then why bother with resolutions along your sorrowful way? Far better to appreciate that we are blessed with a chance at life for however long it lasts, wherein the culmination of our ongoing resolutions end up defining how well or poorly we embraced the most precious destiny imaginable. To live.

So, you see what I am saying, that resolutions are far more meaningful as an ongoing process. I would go farther, despite having no proof of it, to claim those who practice resolutions with such consistency will tend to habitually be kinder to others, quick to jump in and help others, be more apt to outwardly encourage others, and in general come to realize an overall betterment of themselves in the process.

And, yes, I am not blind, during the past couple hundred pages I have taken aim at people among us who make our resolution to sustain staying positive a lot more difficult than need be. And sometimes we are deterred by challenging situations, we are sometimes handed raw deals, but all the hurdles and pitfalls we encounter are most effectively handled by an ongoing resolution to stay upright, optimistic, and most of all, thankful.

I am doing all those things as I close this out, eager to awaken tomorrow and type out the new title page: *Retiree's Diary—Year 2025* and set forth again.

An oddity I have discovered by writing these chronicles, something I could never have seen coming, is the older I get the easier it is to look ahead. Maybe it's because I don't have to strain my eyes, heaven knows there must be some denial mixed in there, but I insist I am living the very best years of my life. That is a superb feeling for a person at any point in life, but especially in later years to be in a good place with oneself epitomizes a life well lived and speaks brightly in defiance of any supposed throwaway trip to a hole in the ground.

Just keep climbing the ladder.

It is always best to end with a laugh, so this year let me bestow the honor to my niece, Wendy Sue, who levied the following coffee-spitter on my Facebook page early one morning. It fits nicely with what we are talking about—to stay in the race and keep climbing the ladder despite whatever impedes your way.

> Me*: I think I'll open this kitchen drawer.*
> Potato Masher*: The hell you will!*

So, yes, sometimes our resolutions meet resistance—nobody denies that; things are not always tidily arranged for smooth sailing, potato mashers seditiously lurking to spoil any scene, but what matters most is to keep answering the million-dollar question: How often do you fail to get that drawer opened?
Right.

—Okay, then; see you tomorrow...

End

Other Books

An Improbable Cast... Called Fishing Partners

A Hunter's Trail—Steps Well Chosen

The Landscape Tamed

Nobody Lied—A Candid Chronicle: Combatting Cancer

Come Cruise the Caribbean

Our Side of The Hill—Modern Rural Life Through The Eyes Of An Intellectual Redneck

Resurgence—A Hunter's Road to Recovery

Good Patina—Ornate Scars from Having Lived—A Memoir

Beyond The Frame—A Photo Album Cast in Words

A Retiree's Diary—Year 2022

A Retiree's Diary—Year 2023